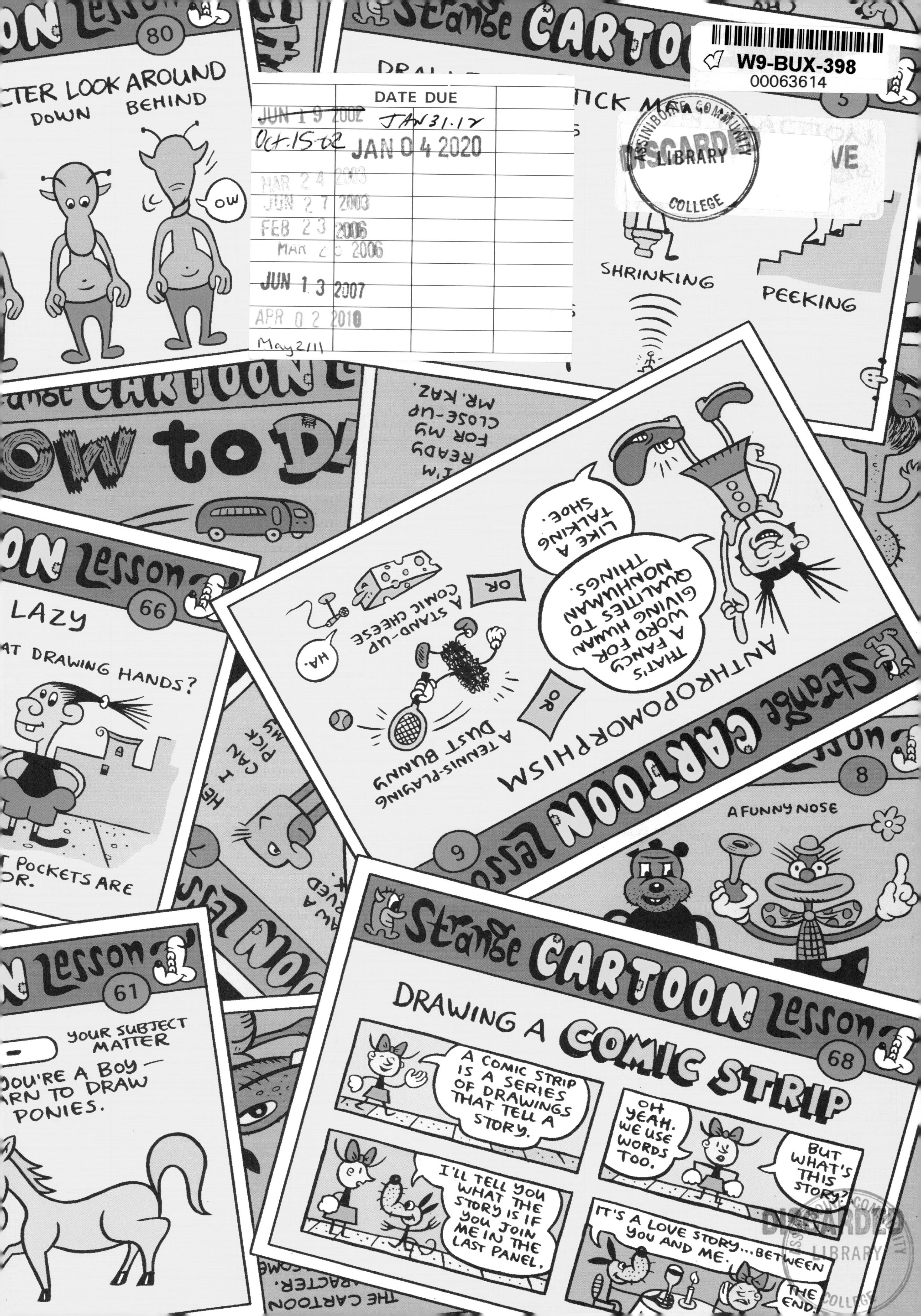

Strange CARTOON Lesson 80
CTER LOOK AROUND
DOWN
BEHIND
OW
Strange CARTOON Lesson 5
SHRINKING
PEEKING
HOW TO D
I'M READY FOR MY CLOSE-UP MR. KAZ.
CARTOON Lesson 66
LAZY
AT DRAWING HANDS?
T POCKETS ARE
OR.
Strange CARTOON Lesson 9
ANTHROPOMORPHISM
THAT'S A FANCY WORD FOR GIVING HUMAN QUALITIES TO NONHUMAN THINGS.
LIKE A TALKING SHOE.
A STAND-UP COMIC CHEESE
HA.
OR
A TENNIS-PLAYING DUST BUNNY
OR
CARTOON Lesson 8
A FUNNY NOSE
CARTOON Lesson 61
YOUR SUBJECT MATTER
OU'RE A BOY—
ARN TO DRAW
PONIES.
Strange CARTOON Lesson 68
DRAWING A COMIC STRIP
A COMIC STRIP IS A SERIES OF DRAWINGS THAT TELL A STORY.
OH YEAH. WE USE WORDS TOO.
BUT WHAT'S THIS STORY?
I'LL TELL YOU WHAT THE STORY IS IF YOU JOIN ME IN THE LAST PANEL.
IT'S A LOVE STORY... BETWEEN YOU AND ME.
THE END.

Little Lit

Strange Stories for Strange Kids

COVER
charles burns

5

THE SEVERAL SELVES OF SELBY SHELDRAKE
art spiegelman

9

ROODY HOOSTER
martin handford

10

CEREAL BABY KELLER
maurice sendak

12

CAN YOU FIND...?
richard mcguire

13

RUNAWAY SHADOW
barbara mcclintock

16

PRETTY UGLY
ian falconer
& david sedaris

21

THE LITTLE HOUSE THAT RAN AWAY FROM HOME
claude ponti

25

TRAPPED IN A COMIC BOOK
jules feiffer

A RAW Junior Book

E D I T E D   B Y

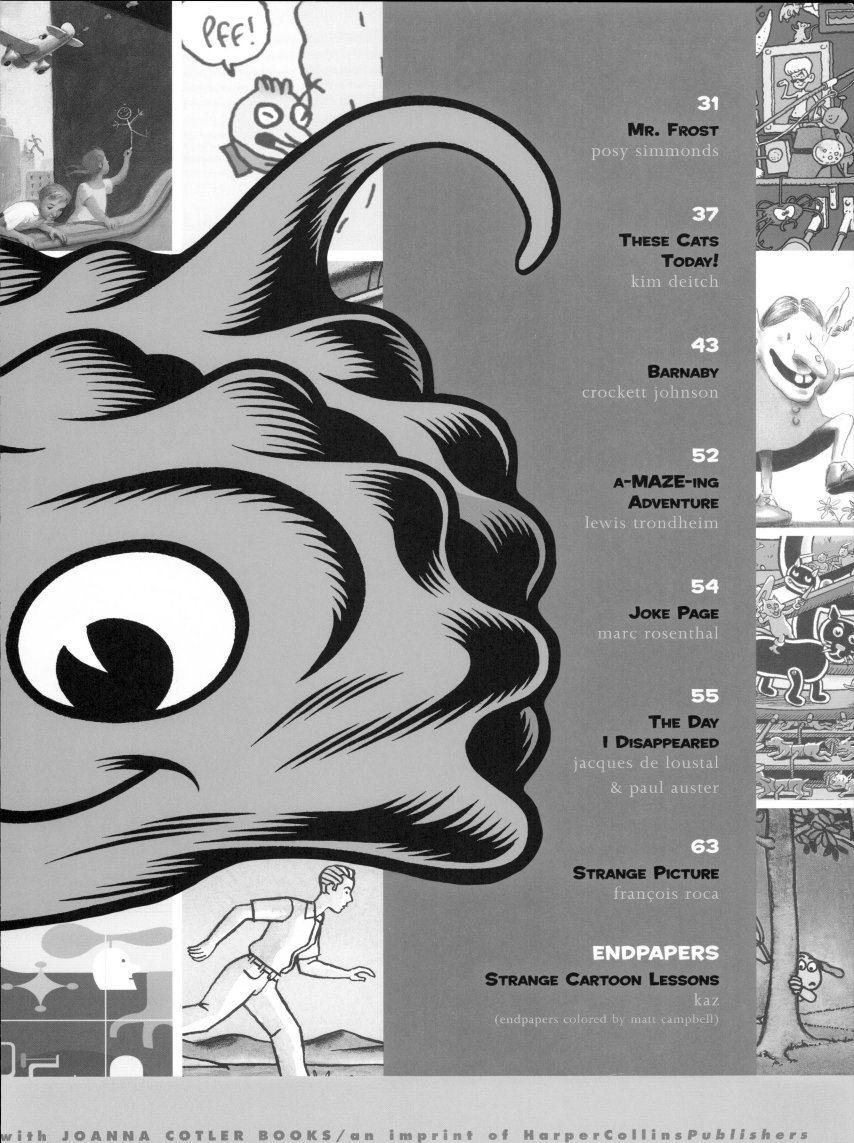

31
MR. FROST
posy simmonds

37
THESE CATS TODAY!
kim deitch

43
BARNABY
crockett johnson

52
A-MAZE-ING ADVENTURE
lewis trondheim

54
JOKE PAGE
marc rosenthal

55
THE DAY I DISAPPEARED
jacques de loustal
& paul auster

63
STRANGE PICTURE
françois roca

ENDPAPERS
STRANGE CARTOON LESSONS
kaz
(endpapers colored by matt campbell)

with JOANNA COTLER BOOKS/an imprint of HarperCollinsPublishers

ART SPIEGELMAN & FRANÇOISE MOULY

designed by FRANÇOISE MOULY and ART SPIEGELMAN

dedicated to DASHIELL and NADJA

editorial associate:
NOVA REN SUMA

production:
NOVA REN SUMA
FRANÇOISE MOULY

with grateful thanks to:
GREG CAPTAIN
LEE HEYDOLPH
MARK MICHAELSON

For information write to HarperCollins Children's Books, a division of HarperCollins Publishers Inc., 1350 Avenue of the Americas, New York, NY 10019. www.harperchildrens.com. Library of Congress Cataloging-in-Publication Data: Little Lit : Strange Stories for Strange Kids /edited by Art Spiegelman & Françoise Mouly. p.cm.– (Little Lit ;2) "A RAW Junior book with Joanna Cotler books." ISBN 0-06-028626-1 [1. Cartoons and comics. 2. Short Stories.] I. Spiegelman, Art. II. Mouly, Françoise. PN6726.L58 2001 741.5'973—dc21 00-067147.
Printed in China by Oceanic Graphic Printing.
10 9 8
7 6 5
4 3
2
1

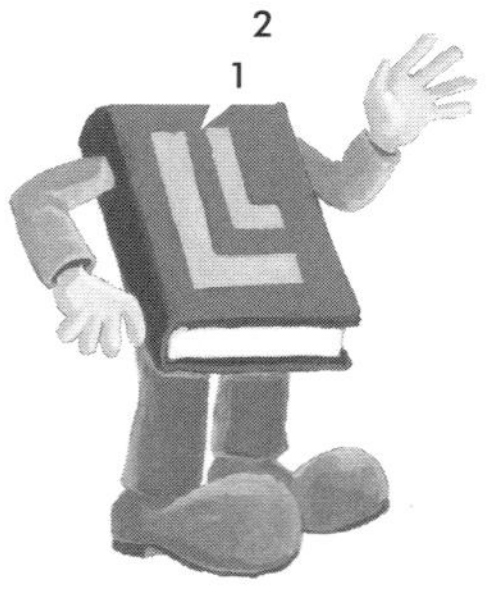

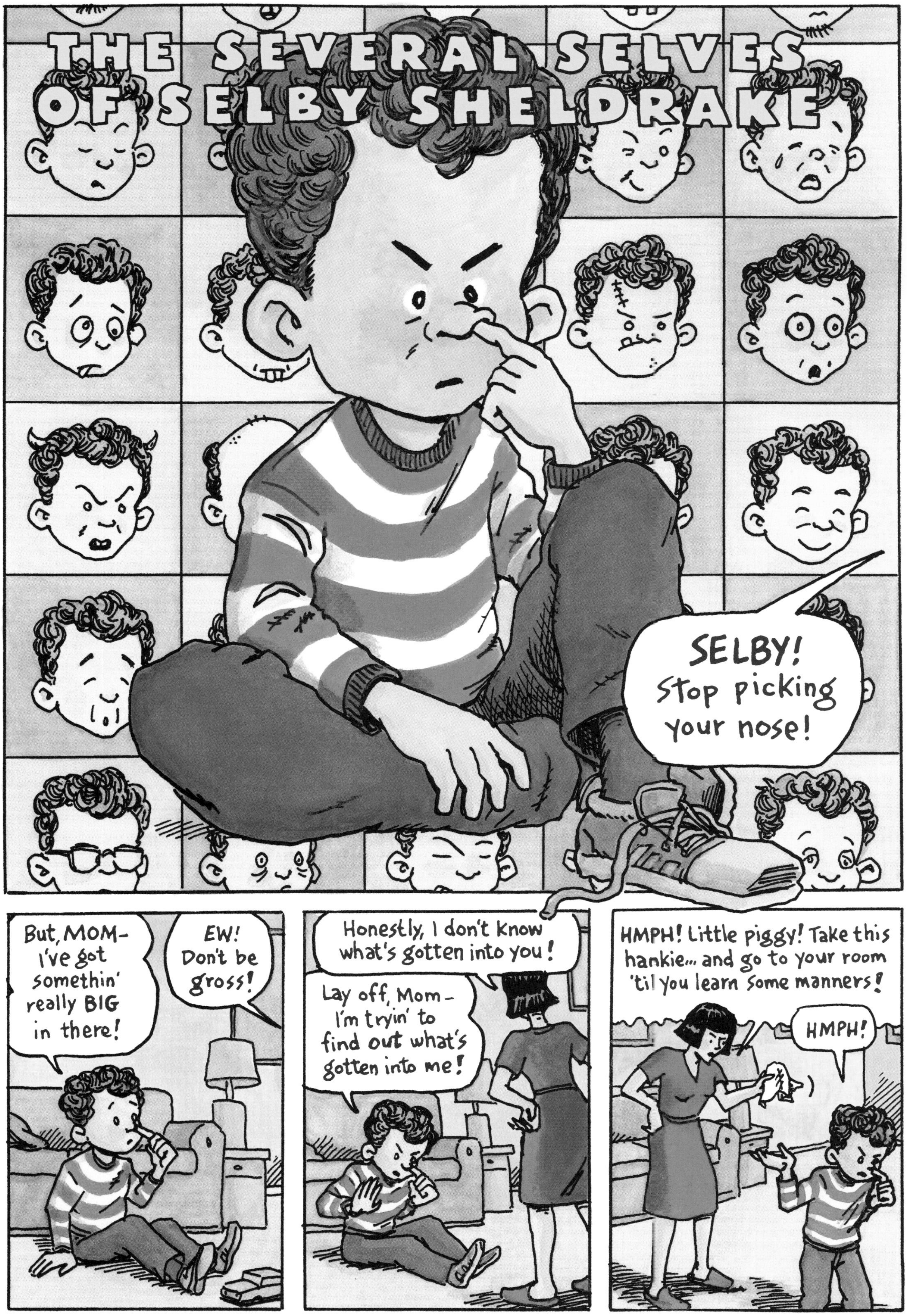
THE SEVERAL SELVES OF SELBY SHELDRAKE
SELBY! Stop picking your nose!
But, MOM- I've got somethin' really BIG in there!
EW! Don't be gross!
Honestly, I don't know what's gotten into you!
Lay off, Mom- I'm tryin' to find out what's gotten into me!
HMPH! Little piggy! Take this hankie... and go to your room 'til you learn some manners!
HMPH!

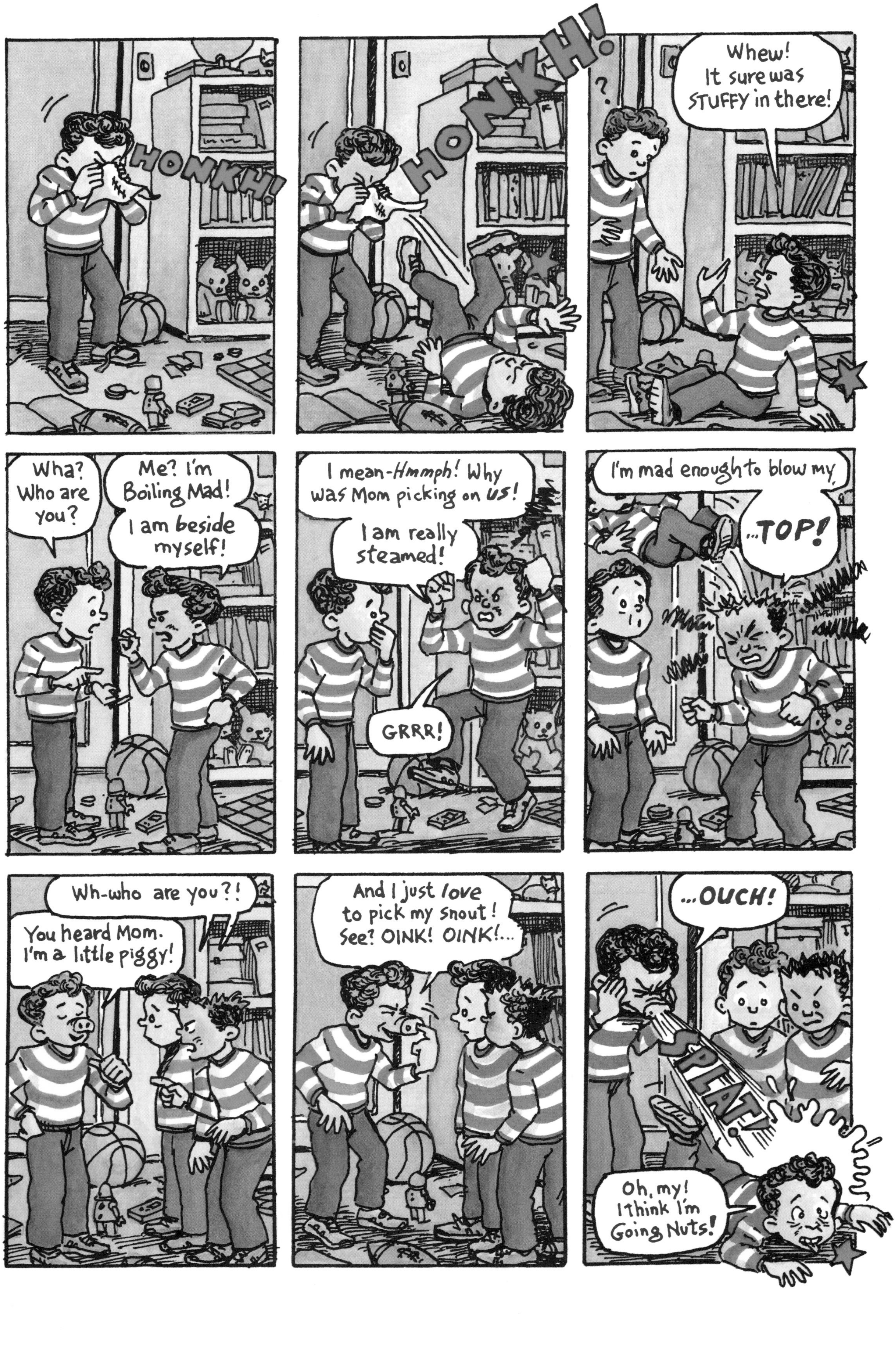
HONKH!
HONKH!
?
Whew! It sure was STUFFY in there!
Wha? Who are you?
Me? I'm Boiling Mad!
I am beside myself!
I mean-Hmmph! Why was Mom picking on US!
I am really steamed!
GRRR!
I'm mad enough to blow my
...TOP!
Wh-who are you?!
You heard Mom. I'm a little piggy!
And I just love to pick my snout! See? OINK! OINK!...
...OUCH!
SPLAT!
Oh, my! I think I'm Going Nuts!

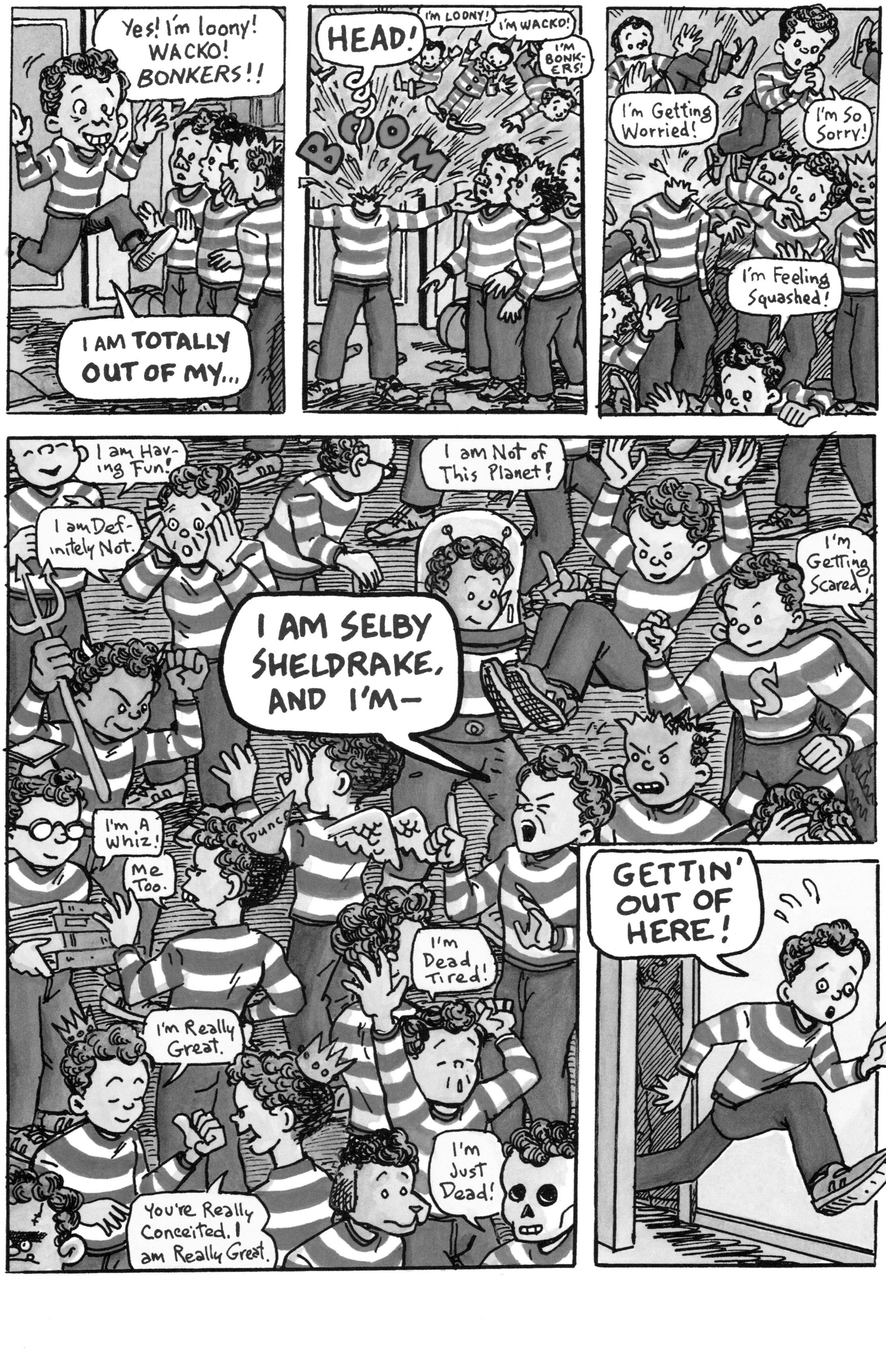
Yes! I'm loony! WACKO! BONKERS!!
I AM TOTALLY OUT OF MY...
HEAD!
BOOM
I'M LOONY!
I'M WACKO!
I'M BONKERS!
I'm Getting Worried!
I'm So Sorry!
I'm Feeling Squashed!
I am Having Fun!
I am Definitely Not.
I am Not of This Planet!
I'm Getting Scared!
I AM SELBY SHELDRAKE, AND I'M—
I'm A Whiz!
Me Too.
DUNCE
I'm Dead Tired!
I'm Really Great.
I'm Just Dead!
You're Really Conceited. I am Really Great.
GETTIN' OUT OF HERE!

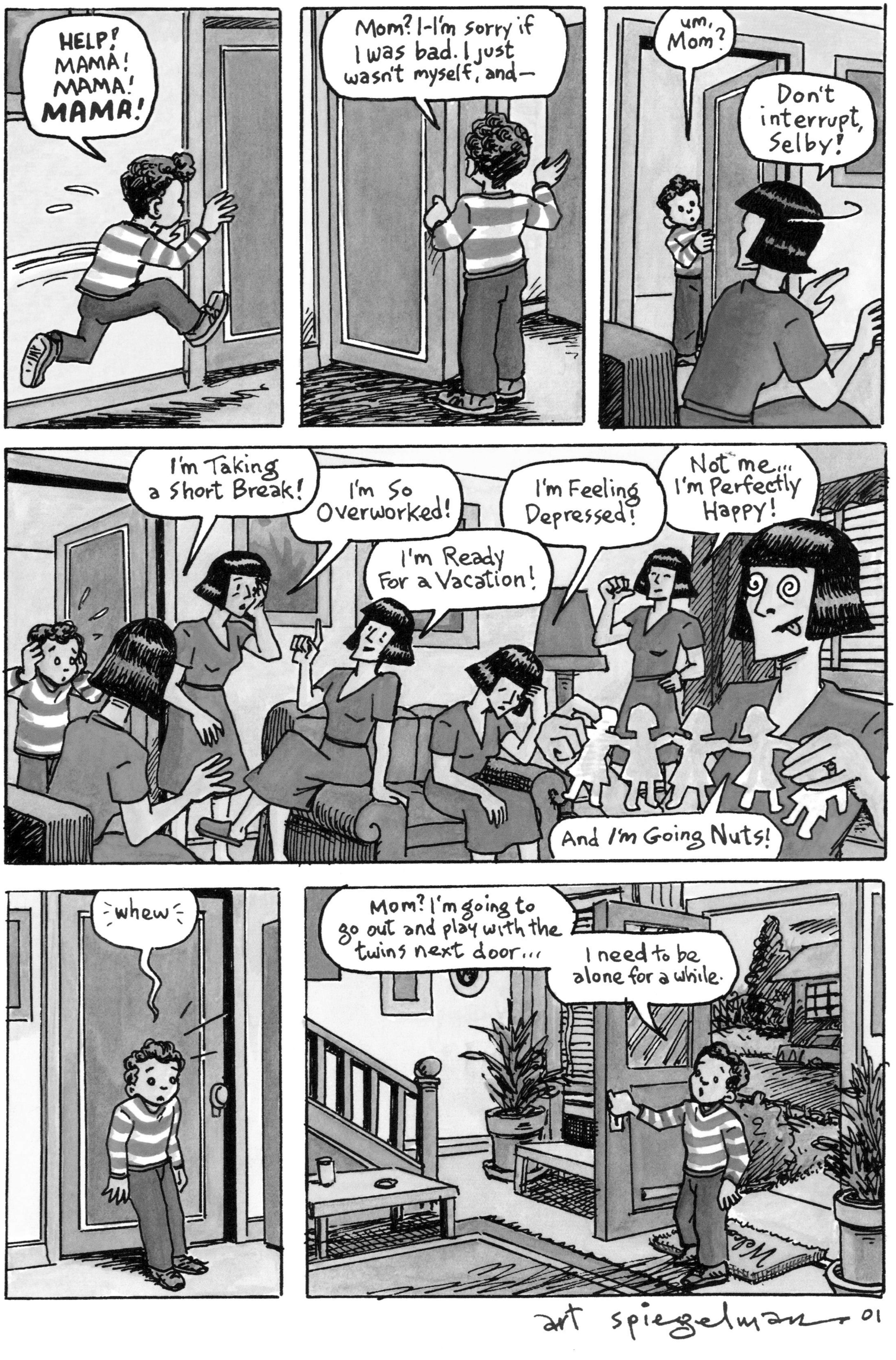
HELP! MAMA! MAMA! MAMA!
Mom? I-I'm sorry if I was bad. I just wasn't myself, and—
um, Mom?
Don't interrupt, Selby!
I'm Taking a Short Break!
I'm So Overworked!
I'm Ready For a Vacation!
I'm Feeling Depressed!
Not me... I'm Perfectly Happy!
And I'm Going Nuts!
whew
Mom? I'm going to go out and play with the twins next door...
I need to be alone for a while.
art spiegelman 01

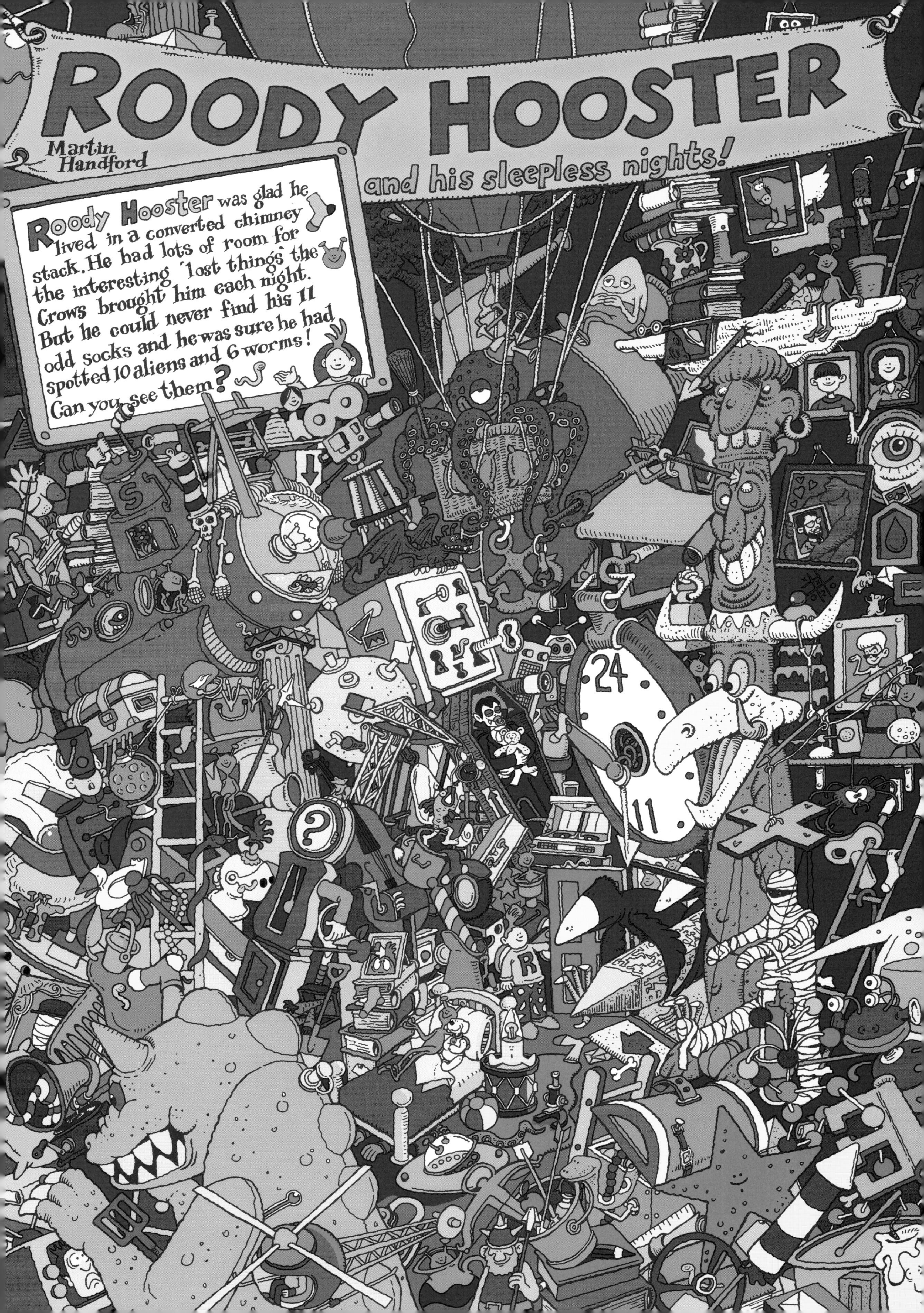
ROODY HOOSTER
Martin Handford
and his sleepless nights!
Roody Hooster was glad he lived in a converted chimney stack. He had lots of room for the interesting 'lost things' the Crows brought him each night. But he could never find his 11 odd socks and he was sure he had spotted 10 aliens and 6 worms! Can you see them?

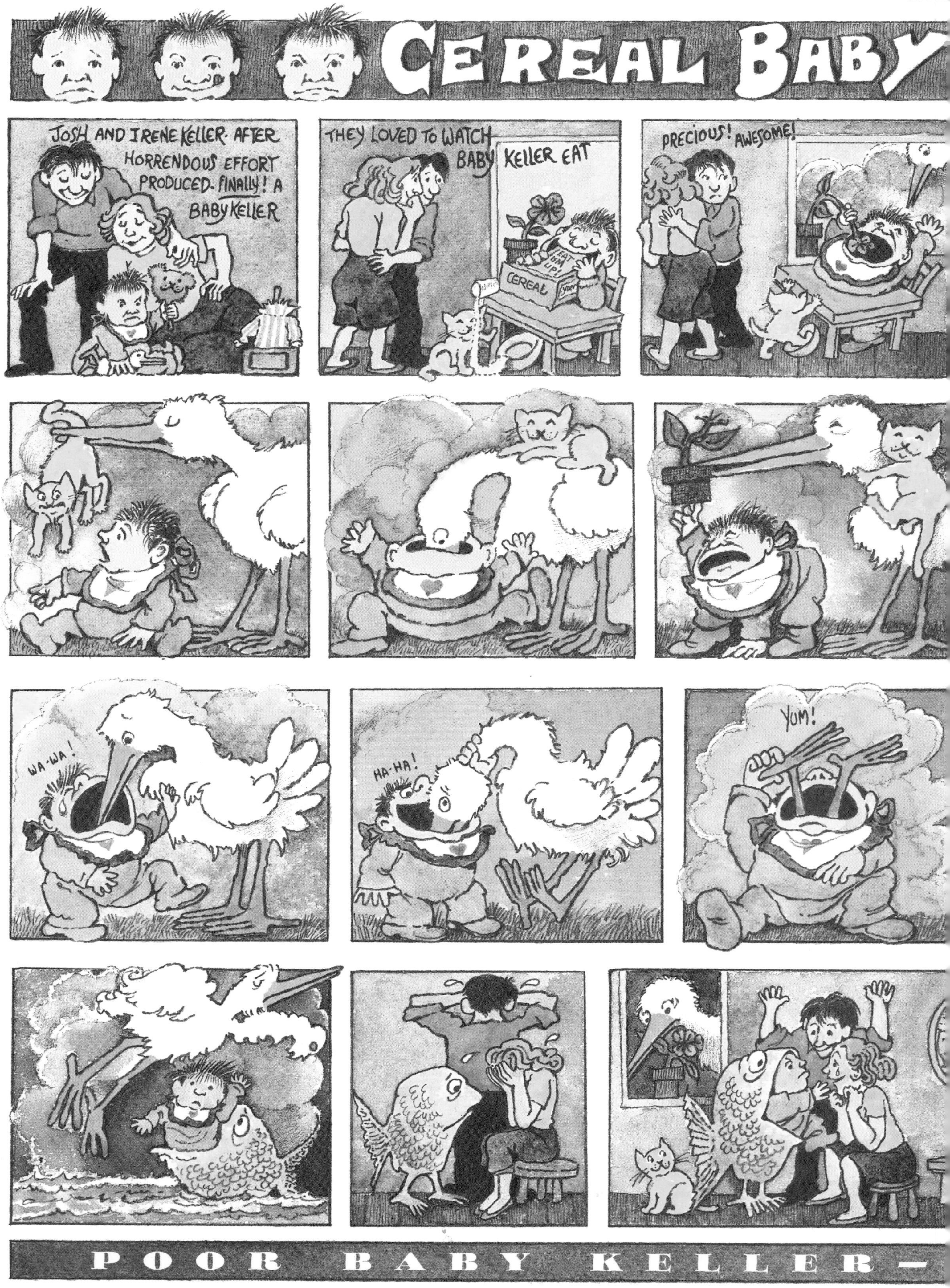
CEREAL BABY
JOSH AND IRENE KELLER · AFTER HORRENDOUS EFFORT PRODUCED · FINALLY! A BABY KELLER
THEY LOVED TO WATCH BABY KELLER EAT
EAT 'EM UP!
CEREAL
PRECIOUS!
AWESOME!
WA-WA!
HA-HA!
YUM!
POOR BABY KELLER —

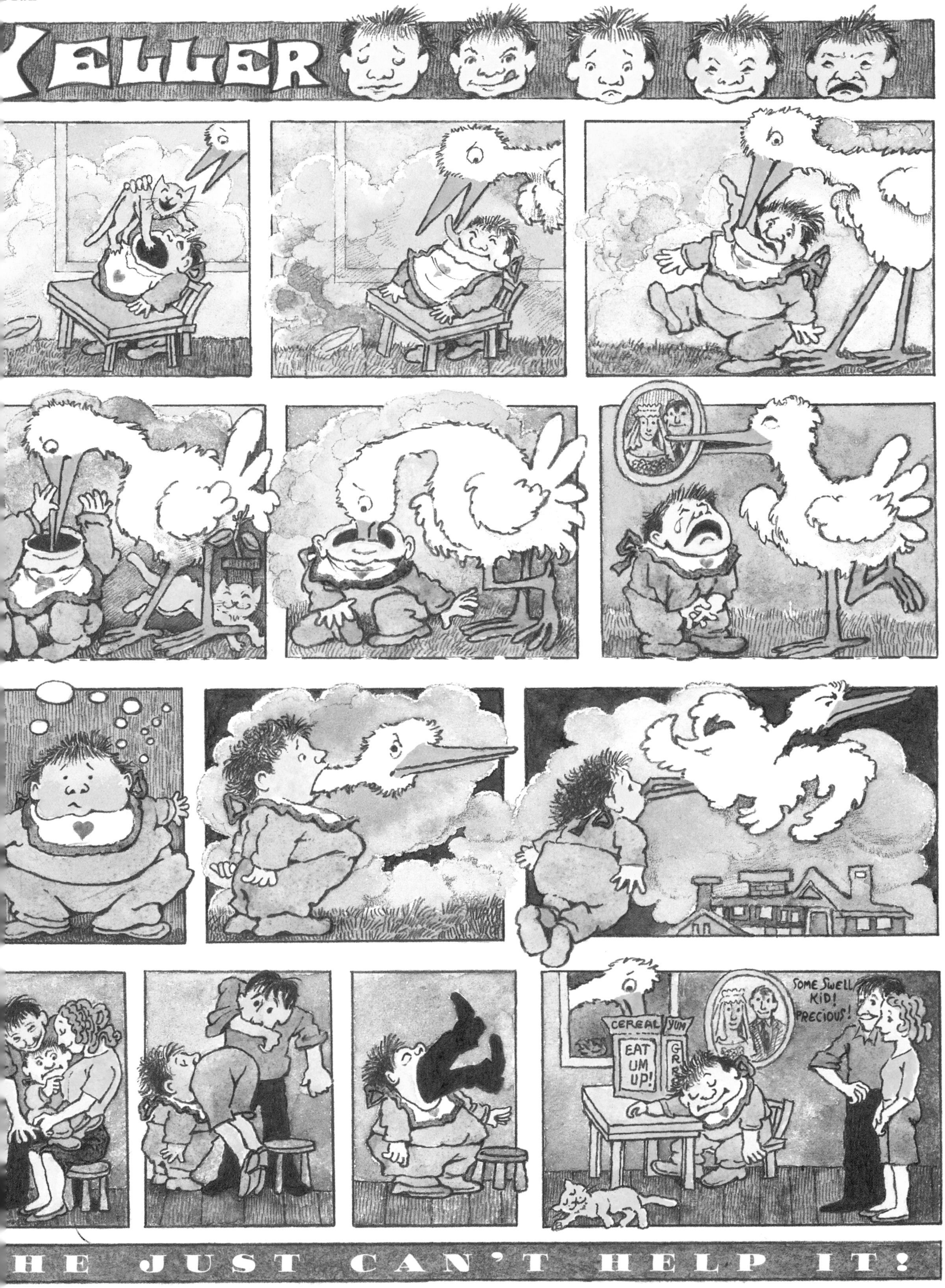
ELLER
CEREAL
YUM
EAT UM UP!
GRR
SOME SWELL KID! PRECIOUS!
HE JUST CAN'T HELP IT!

Maurice Sendak

CAN YOU FIND...

1. Igloo with a Shoe
2. Endless Noodle
3. Floating Sombrero
4. Invisible Egg
5. Rubber Gorilla
6. Snowball with a Nose
7. Runaway Sock & Mitten
8. Frog Disguised as a Rock
9. Big Idea Stuck in a Tree
10. Whispering Ear
11. Asteroid with a Passenger
12. Cloud with a Beard
13. Propeller Head
14. Hiccupping Ghost
15. Shadow of a Donut
16. Unknown Bump

?

RICHARD MCGUIRE

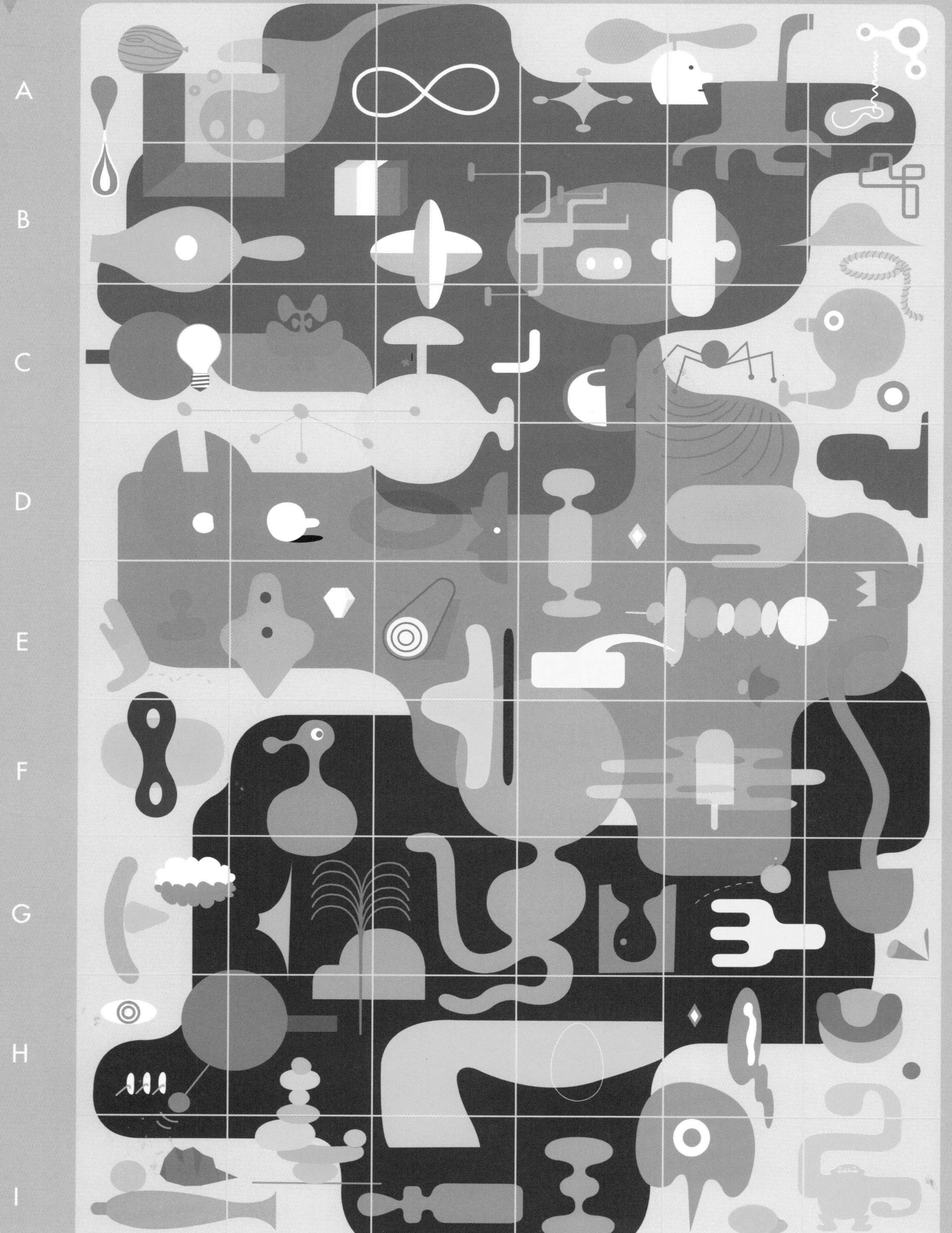

A
B
C
D
E
F
G
H
I
1
2
3
4
5
6

answers

1.C4 \ 2.A3 \ 3.E3+F3 \ 4.H4 \ 5.I6 \ 6.D2 \ 7.E1 \ 8.I1 \ 9.C1 \ 10.A6 \ 11.G5 \ 12.G1 \ 13.A4+A5 \ 14.1A+2A+3A \ 15.D3 \ 16.B6

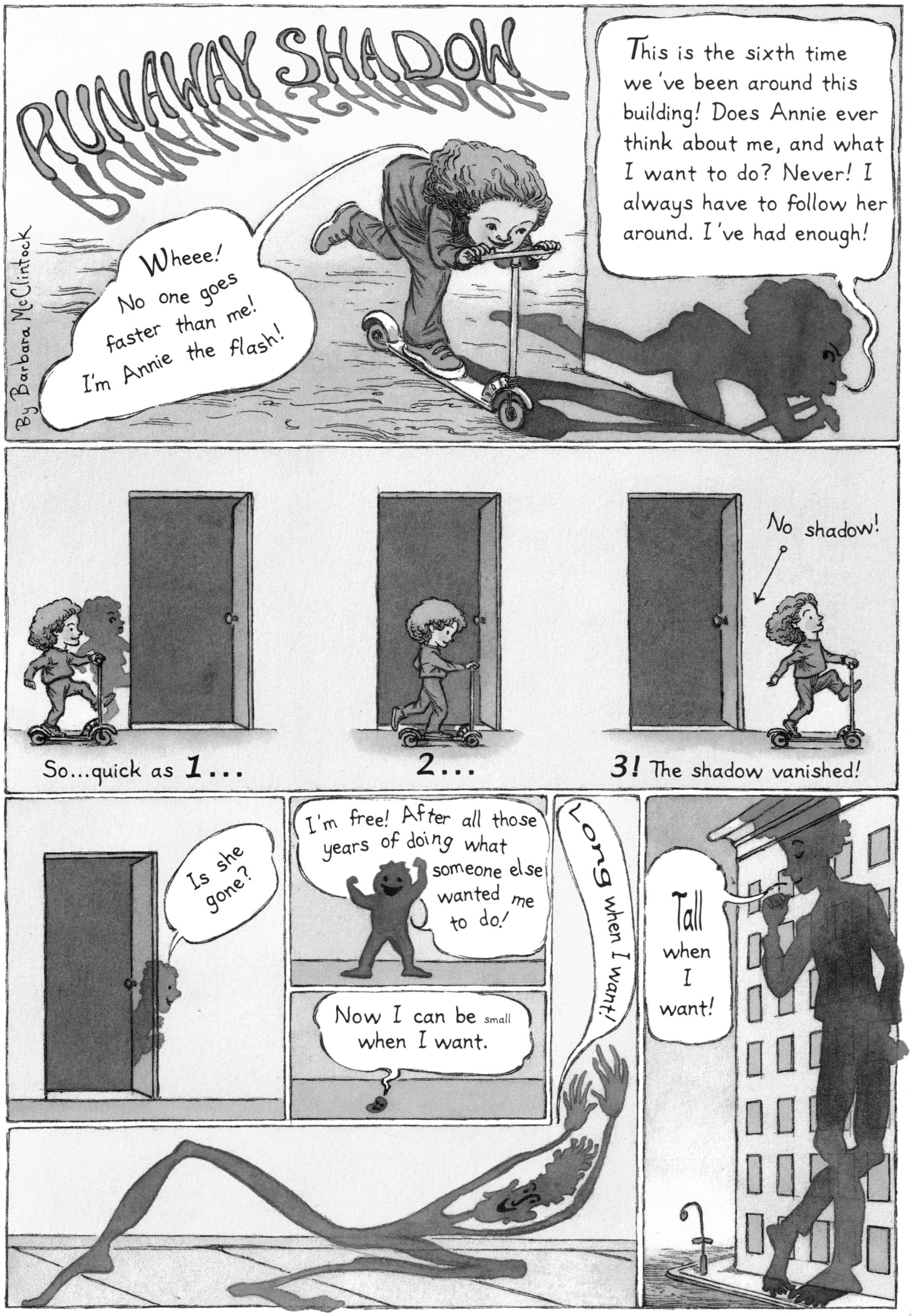
RUNAWAY SHADOW
By Barbara McClintock
Wheee! No one goes faster than me! I'm Annie the flash!
This is the sixth time we've been around this building! Does Annie ever think about me, and what I want to do? Never! I always have to follow her around. I've had enough!
No shadow!
So...quick as 1...
2...
3! The shadow vanished!
Is she gone?
I'm free! After all those years of doing what someone else wanted me to do!
Now I can be small when I want.
Long when I want!
Tall when I want!

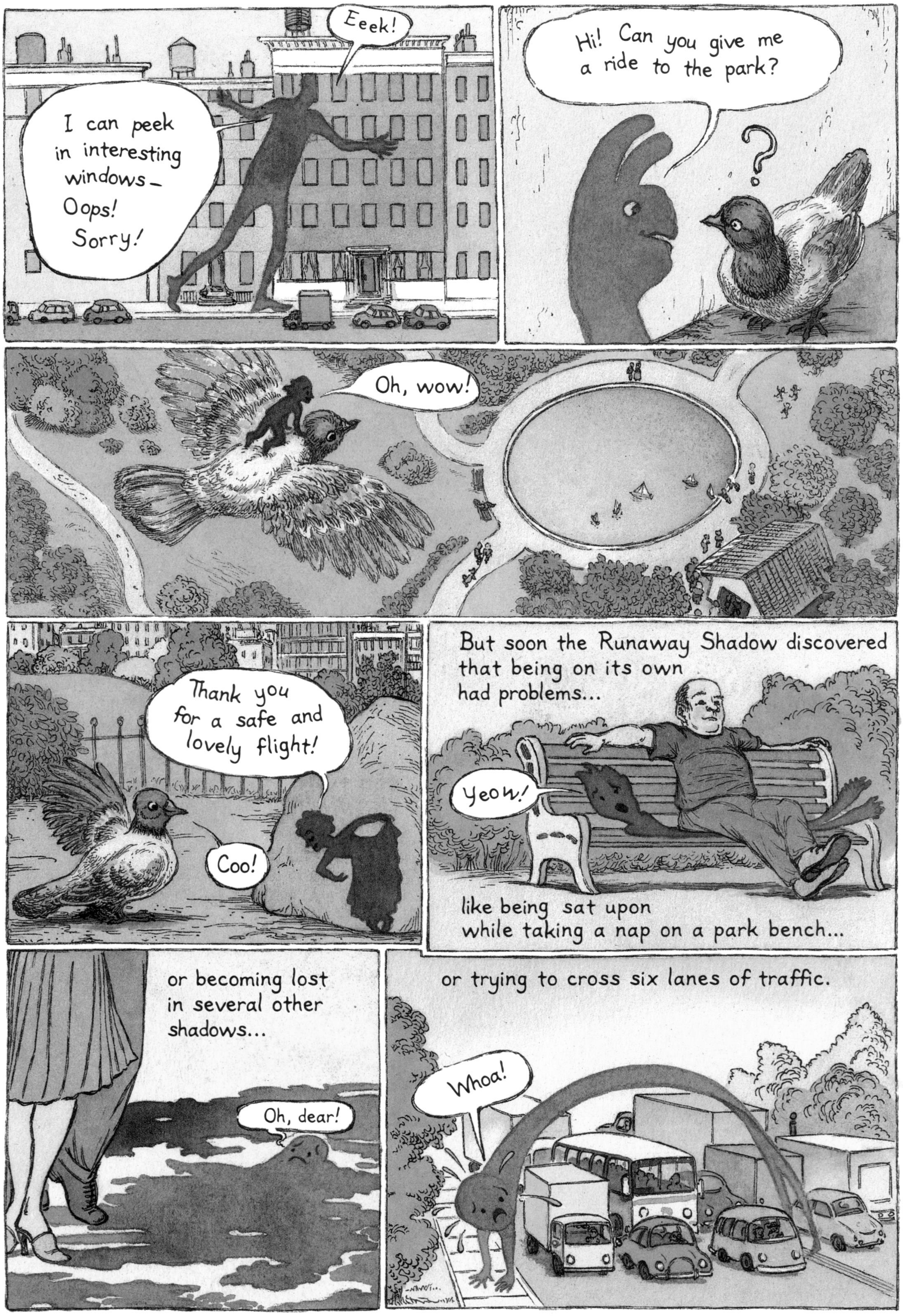
Eeek!
I can peek in interesting windows— Oops! Sorry!
Hi! Can you give me a ride to the park?
?
Oh, wow!
Thank you for a safe and lovely flight!
Coo!
But soon the Runaway Shadow discovered that being on its own had problems...
Yeow!
like being sat upon while taking a nap on a park bench...
or becoming lost in several other shadows...
Oh, dear!
or trying to cross six lanes of traffic.
Whoa!

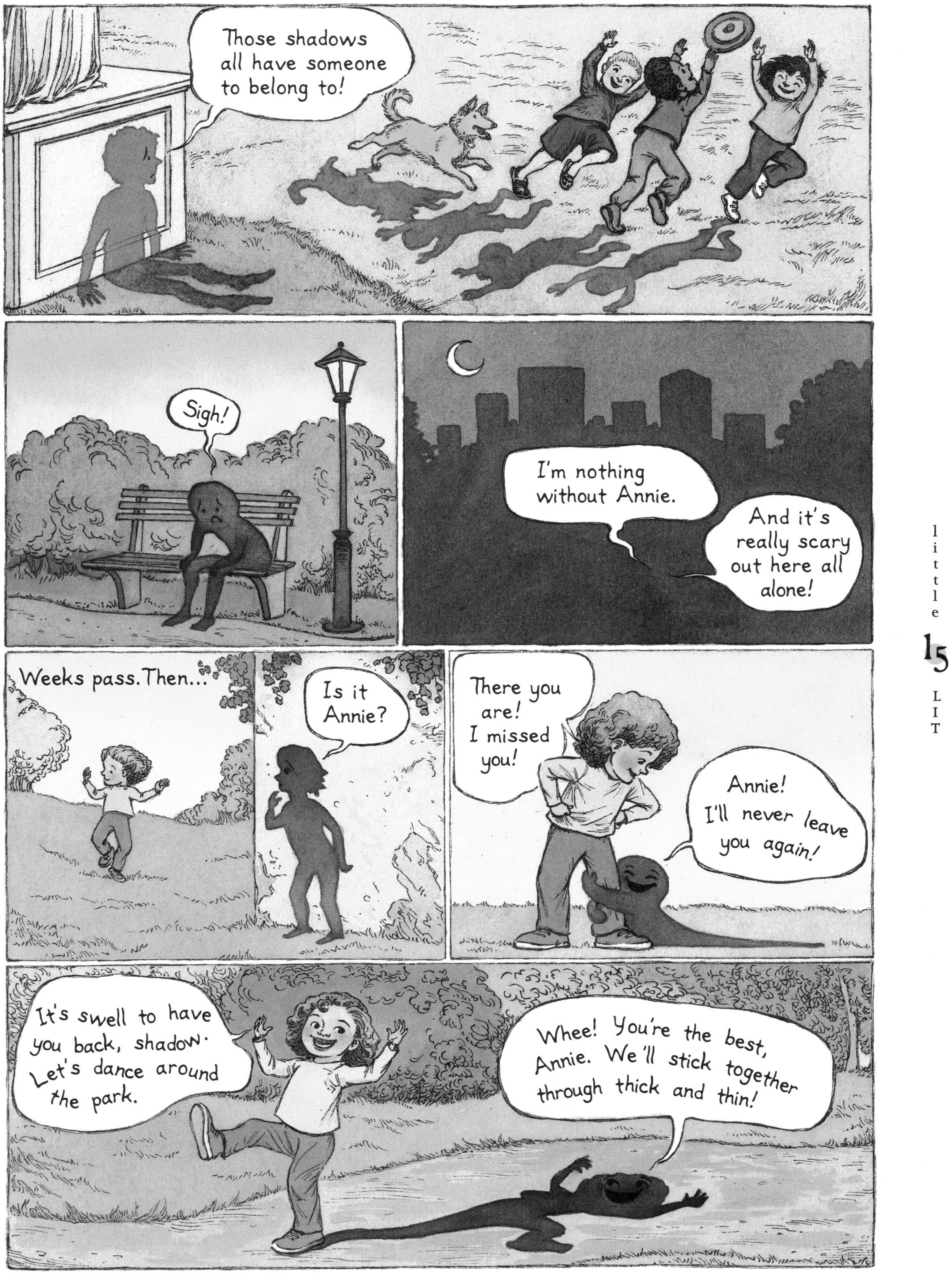
Those shadows all have someone to belong to!
Sigh!
I'm nothing without Annie.
And it's really scary out here all alone!
Weeks pass. Then...
Is it Annie?
There you are! I missed you!
Annie! I'll never leave you again!
It's swell to have you back, shadow. Let's dance around the park.
Whee! You're the best, Annie. We'll stick together through thick and thin!

ian falconer & david sedaris

PRETTY UGLY

When she was good,
Anna Van Ogre...

stomped on the flowers...

threw dirt into the house...

and talked with her mouth full.

These nails is good eatin'.

Thank you, Sweetness.

Isn't she something?

That's our girl.

And when she was bad, Anna made faces, terrible faces...

Look, Grandma, I'm a bunny!

Eeeeeee!

And you'd better be careful, or one day your face will stick like that.

Says who?

Then one day she made the scariest face of all... and it stuck!

Mom, Dad... Grandma... Somebody... I think I need some help!

Her family tried everything... Then they sent her to a doctor who tried everything else...

Folks, I've got some bad news.

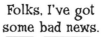

Her family was good about it...

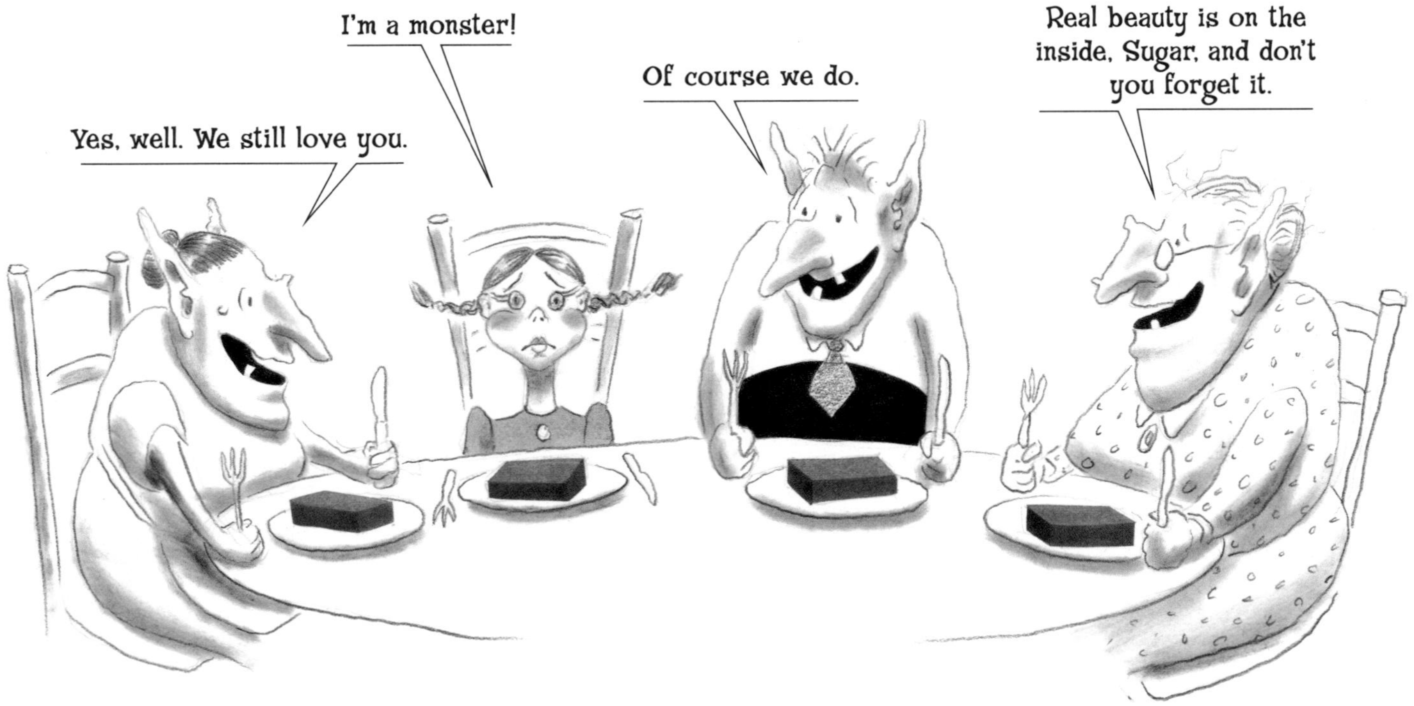
Yes, well. We still love you.
I'm a monster!
Of course we do.
Real beauty is on the inside, Sugar, and don't you forget it.

But outside of the house her life was unbearable...

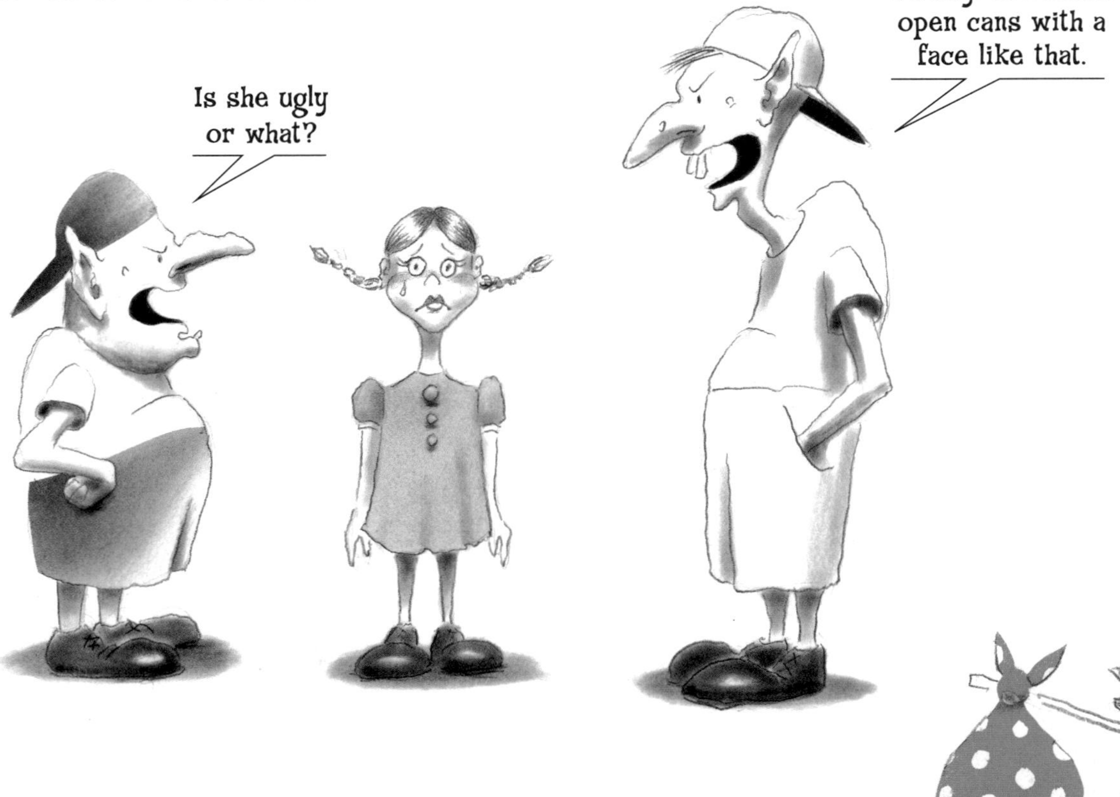
Is she ugly or what?
I'll say. You could open cans with a face like that.

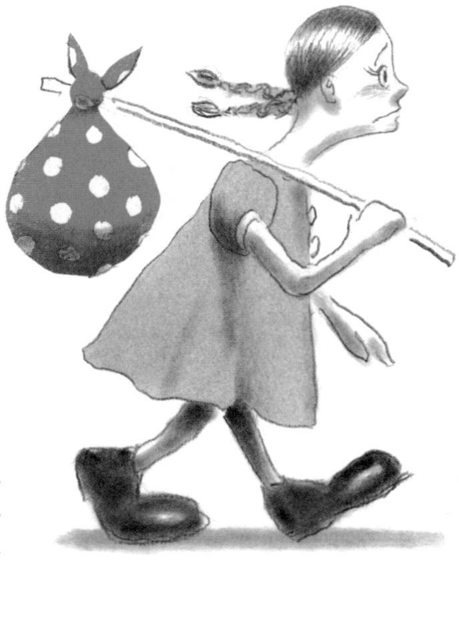

When she could stand it no longer, Anna packed a few thumbtack sandwiches and locked herself in the woodshed.

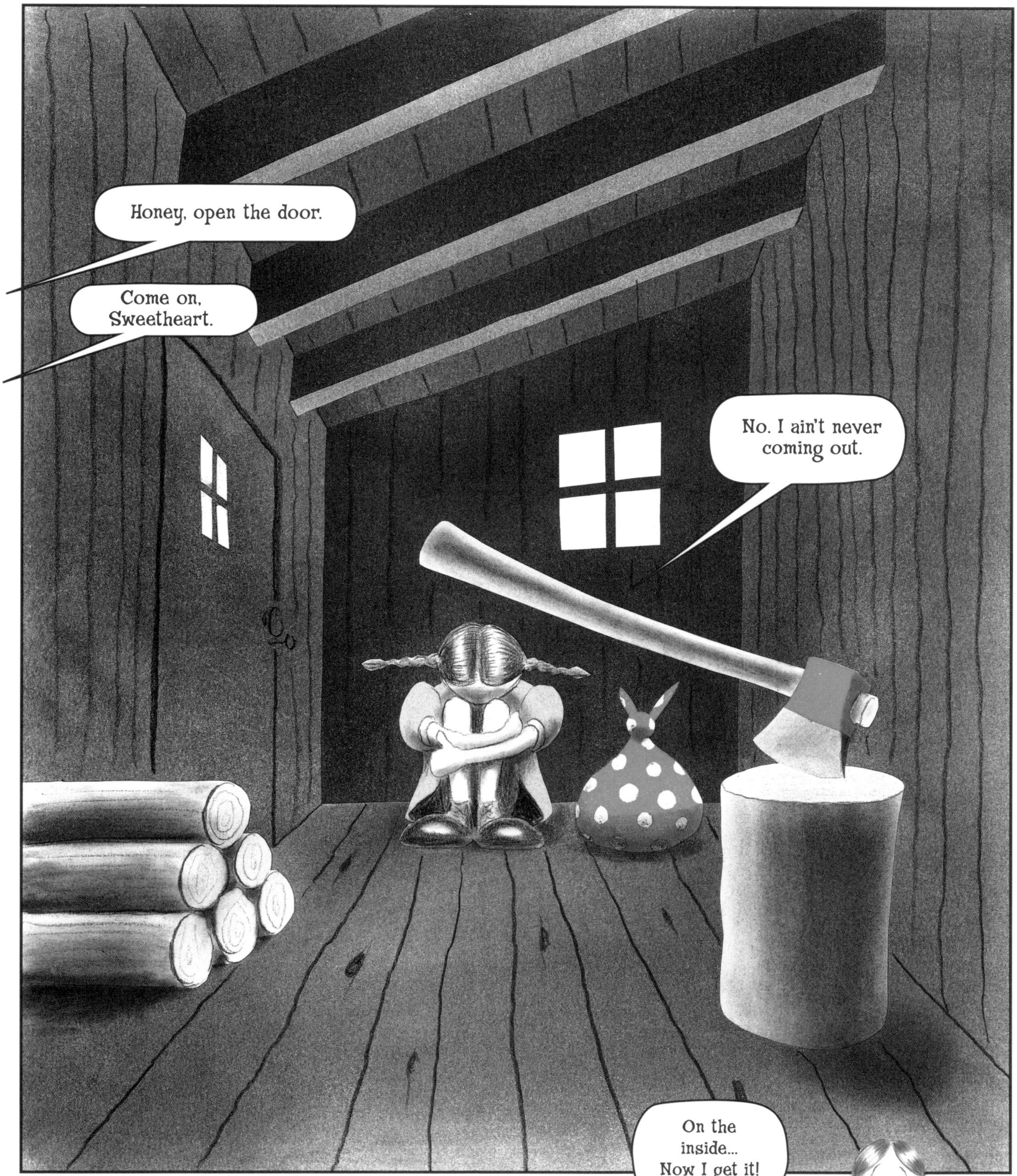

Honey, open the door.
Come on, Sweetheart.
No. I ain't never coming out.

She stayed for three days and three nights, thinking all the while of what her grandmother had said.

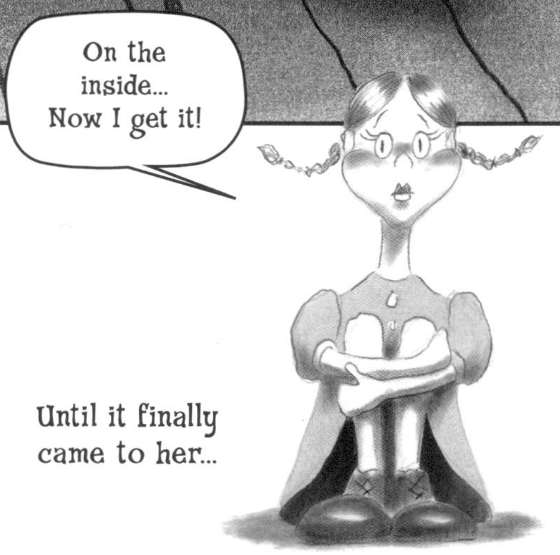

On the inside... Now I get it!

Until it finally came to her...

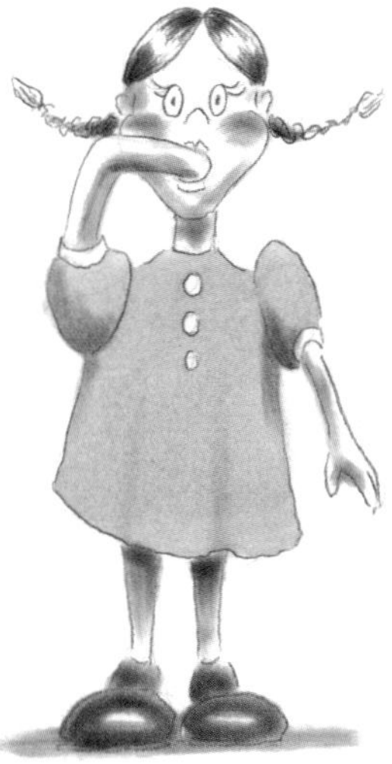

She stuck her hand down her throat...

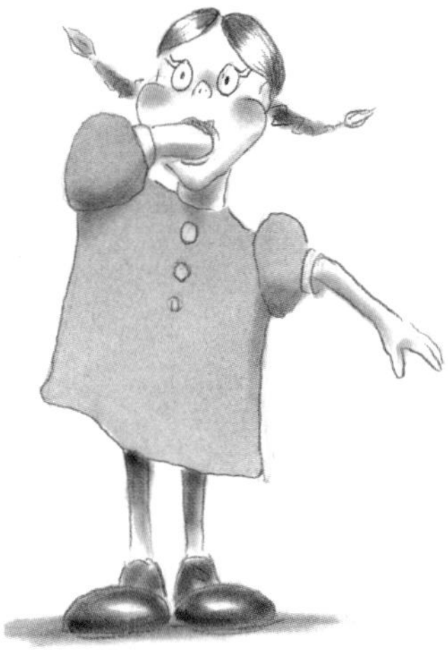

as far as it could go...

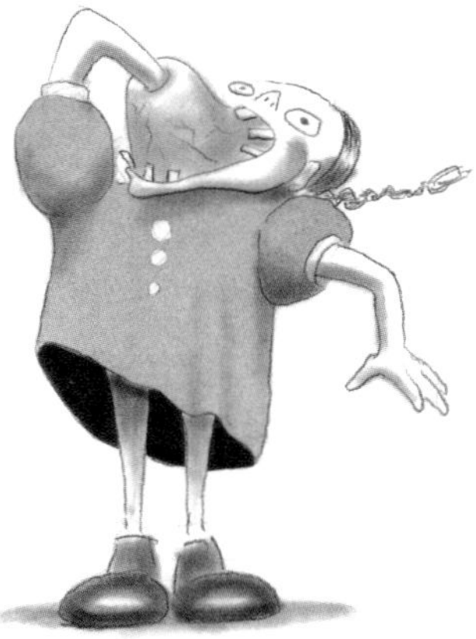

and she yanked...

until she'd turned
herself inside out...
and was beautiful
again.

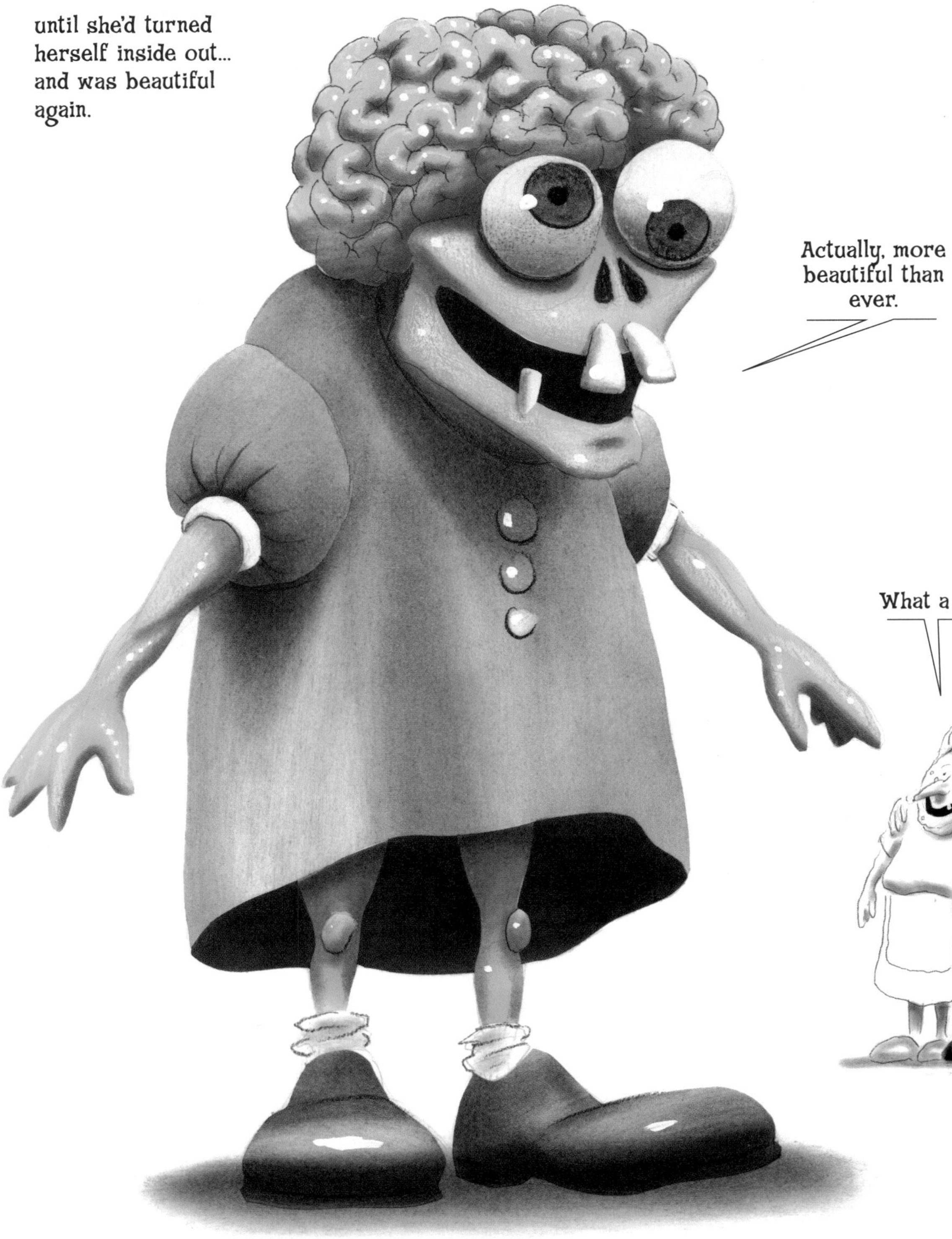
Actually, more beautiful than ever.

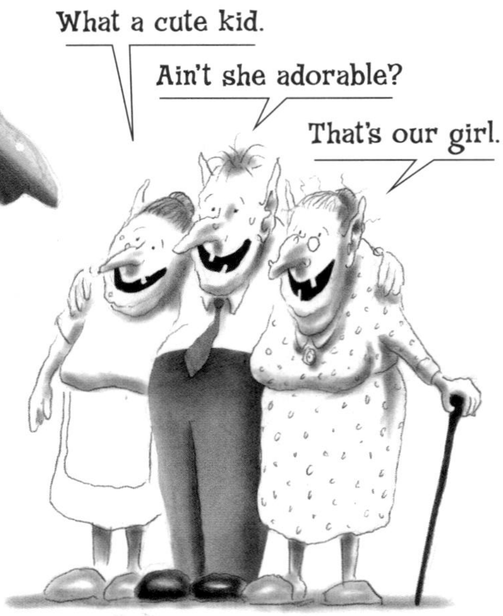
What a cute kid.
Ain't she adorable?
That's our girl.

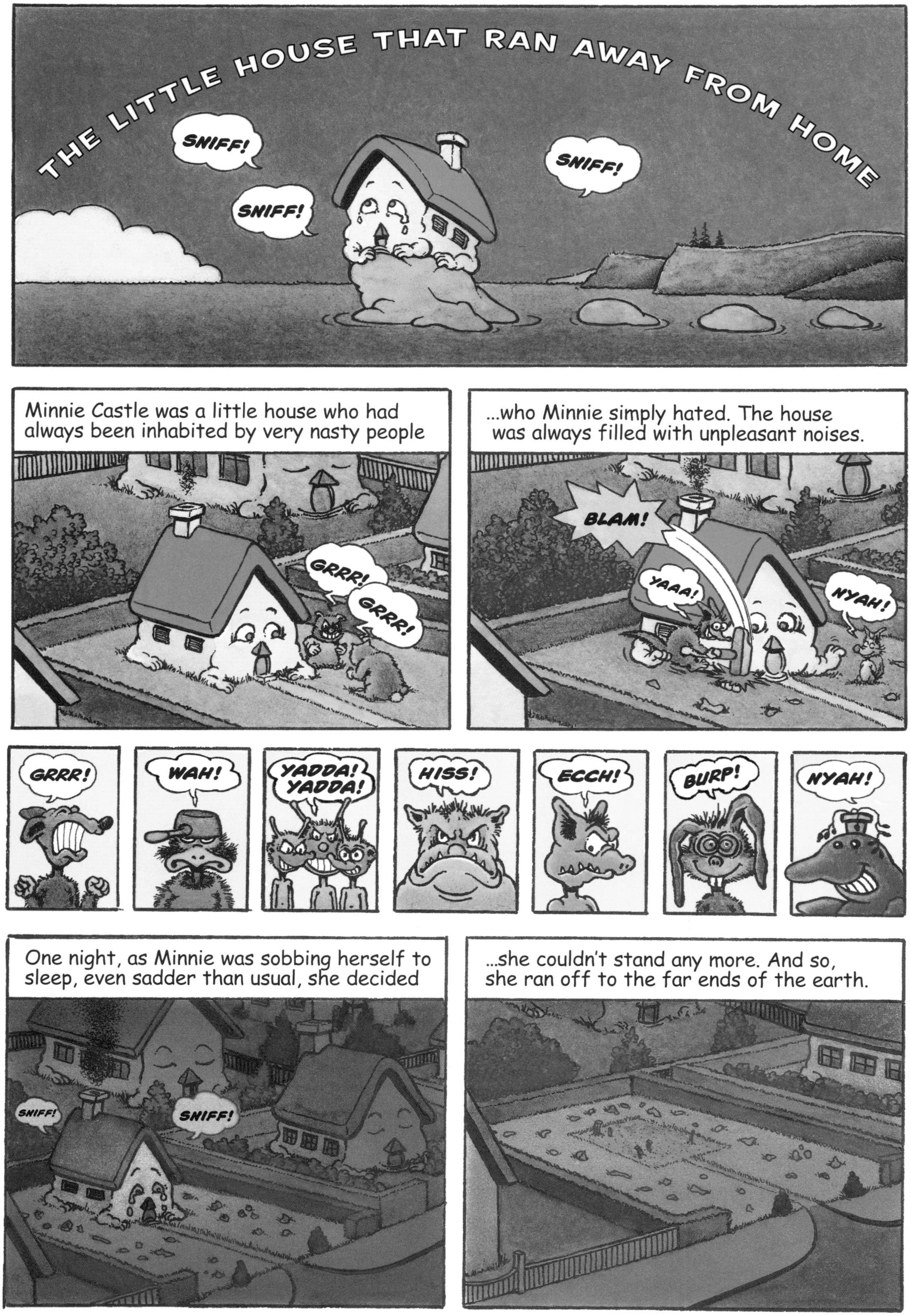
THE LITTLE HOUSE THAT RAN AWAY FROM HOME
SNIFF!
SNIFF!
SNIFF!
Minnie Castle was a little house who had always been inhabited by very nasty people
GRRR!
GRRR!
...who Minnie simply hated. The house was always filled with unpleasant noises.
BLAM!
YAAA!
NYAH!
GRRR!
WAH!
YADDA! YADDA!
HISS!
ECCH!
BURP!
NYAH!
One night, as Minnie was sobbing herself to sleep, even sadder than usual, she decided
SNIFF!
SNIFF!
...she couldn't stand any more. And so, she ran off to the far ends of the earth.

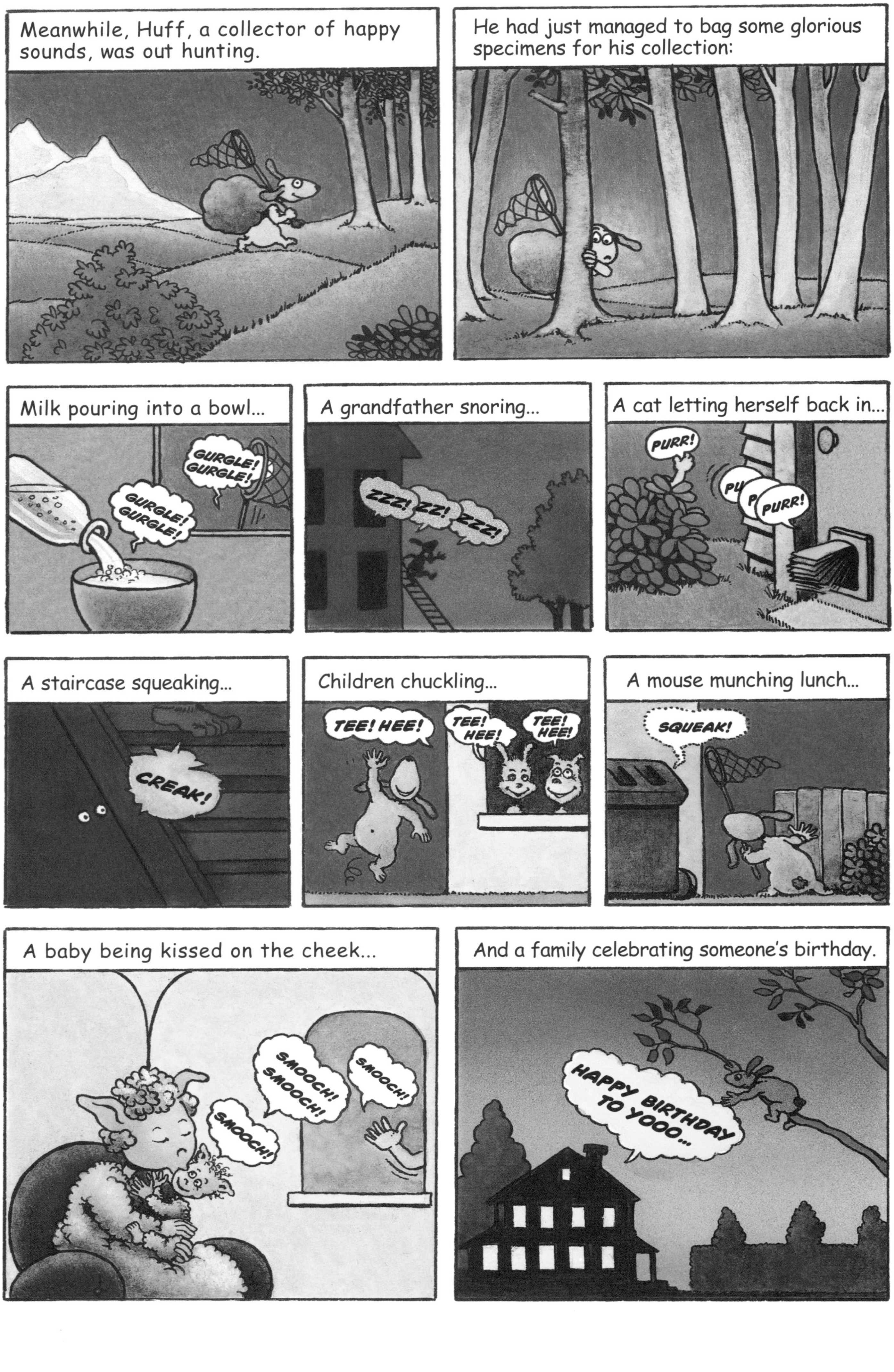
Meanwhile, Huff, a collector of happy sounds, was out hunting.
He had just managed to bag some glorious specimens for his collection:
Milk pouring into a bowl...
GURGLE! GURGLE!
GURGLE! GURGLE!
A grandfather snoring...
ZZZ! ZZ! ZZZ!
A cat letting herself back in...
PURR!
PURR!
A staircase squeaking...
CREAK!
Children chuckling...
TEE! HEE!
TEE! HEE!
TEE! HEE!
A mouse munching lunch...
SQUEAK!
A baby being kissed on the cheek...
SMOOCH! SMOOCH!
SMOOCH!
SMOOCH!
And a family celebrating someone's birthday.
HAPPY BIRTHDAY TO YOOO...

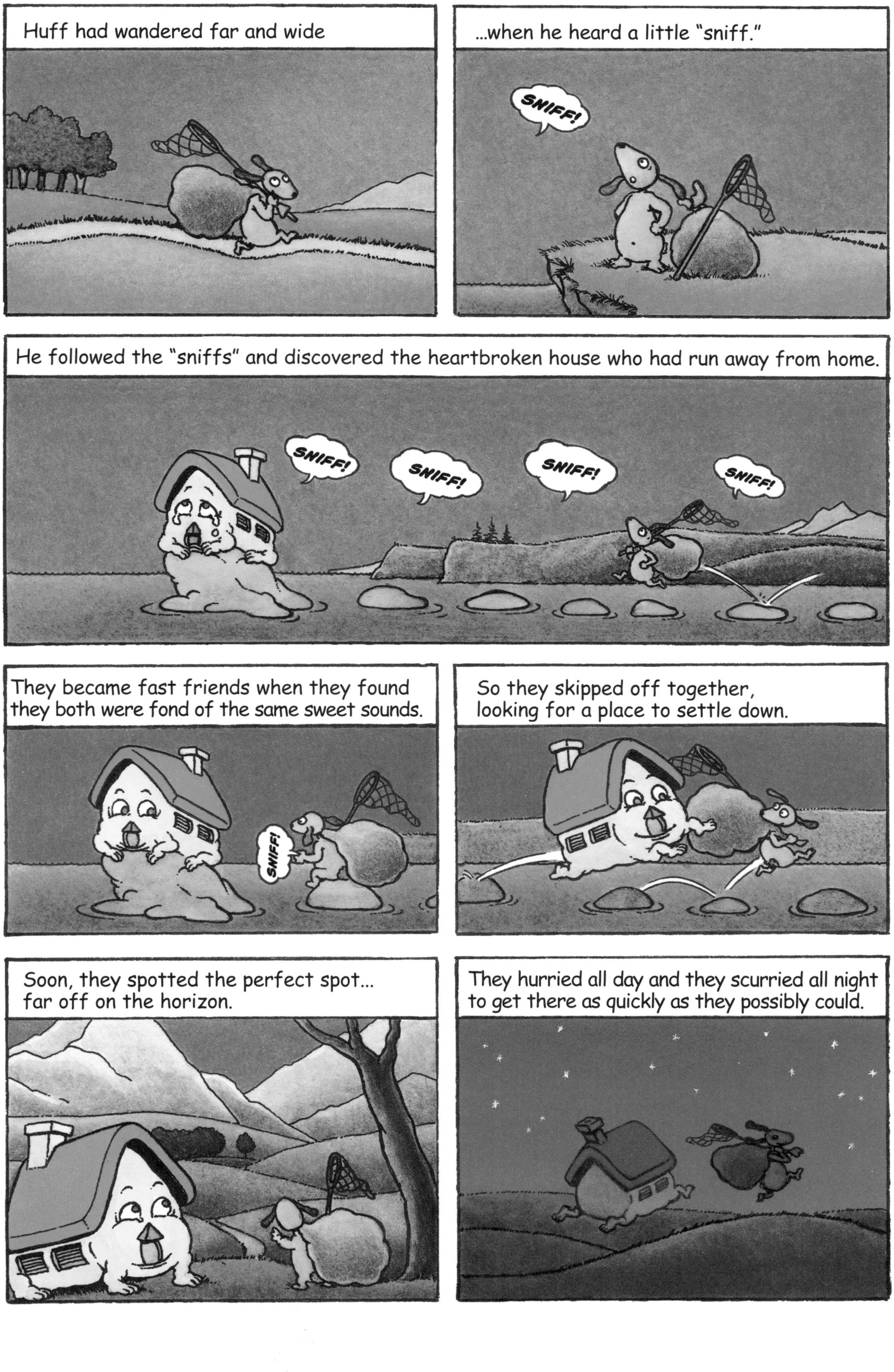
Huff had wandered far and wide
...when he heard a little "sniff."
SNIFF!
He followed the "sniffs" and discovered the heartbroken house who had run away from home.
SNIFF!
SNIFF!
SNIFF!
SNIFF!
They became fast friends when they found they both were fond of the same sweet sounds.
SNIFF!
So they skipped off together, looking for a place to settle down.
Soon, they spotted the perfect spot... far off on the horizon.
They hurried all day and they scurried all night to get there as quickly as they possibly could.

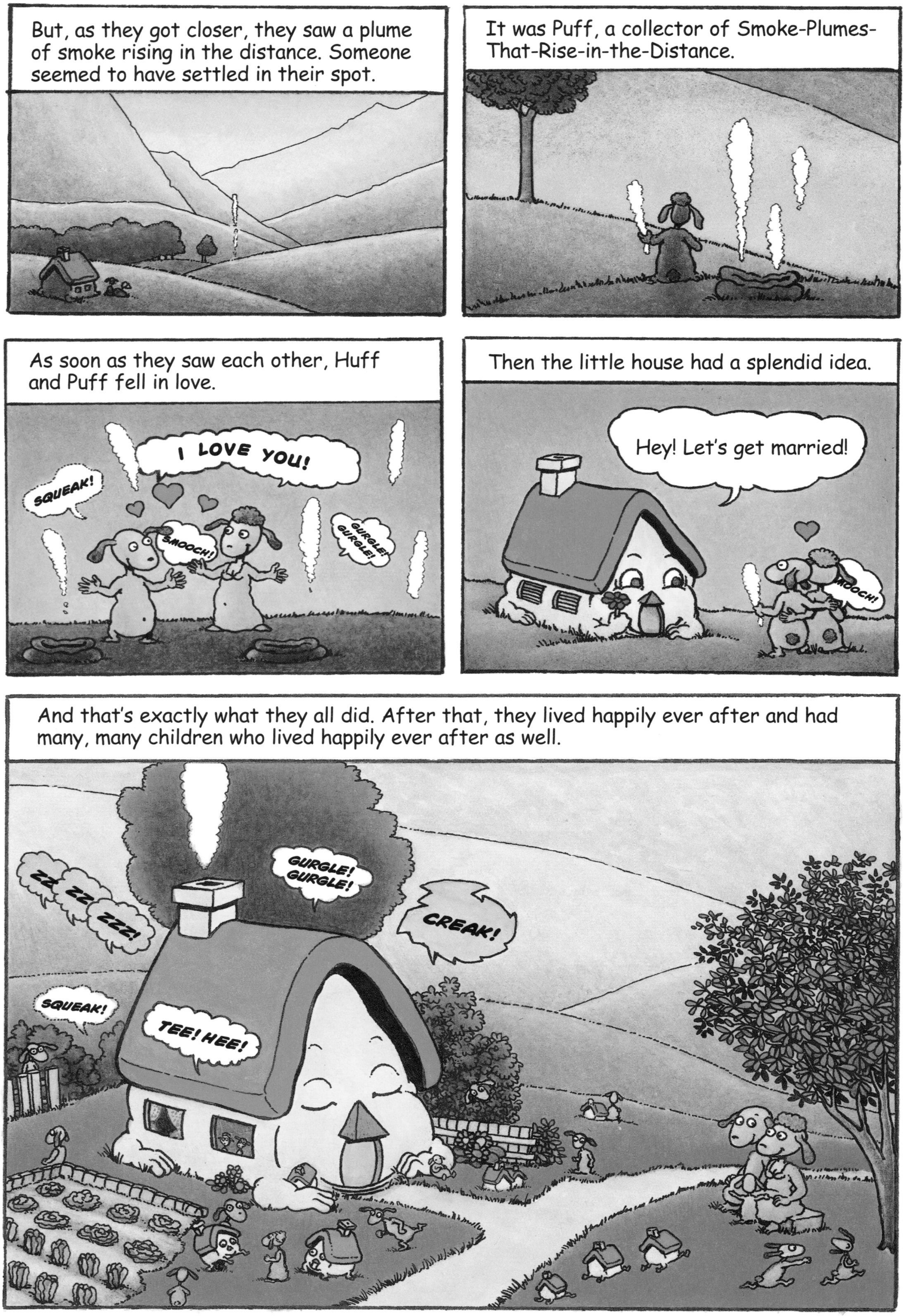
But, as they got closer, they saw a plume of smoke rising in the distance. Someone seemed to have settled in their spot.
It was Puff, a collector of Smoke-Plumes-That-Rise-in-the-Distance.
As soon as they saw each other, Huff and Puff fell in love.
SQUEAK!
I LOVE YOU!
SMOOCH!
GURGLE! GURGLE!
Then the little house had a splendid idea.
Hey! Let's get married!
MOOCH!
And that's exactly what they all did. After that, they lived happily ever after and had many, many children who lived happily ever after as well.
ZZ
ZZ
ZZZ!
GURGLE! GURGLE!
CREAK!
SQUEAK!
TEE! HEE!

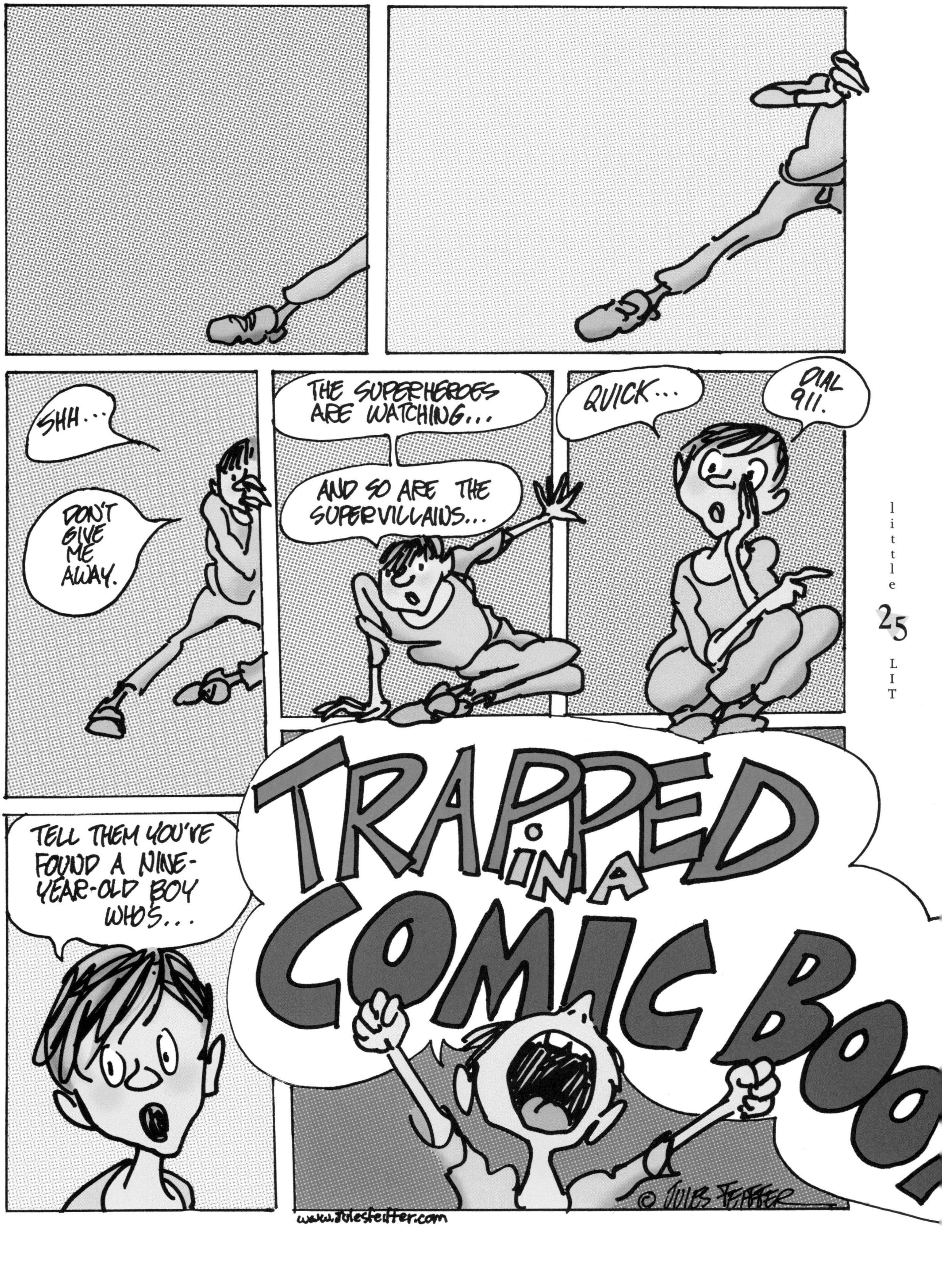
SHH...
DON'T GIVE ME AWAY.
THE SUPERHEROES ARE WATCHING...
AND SO ARE THE SUPERVILLAINS...
QUICK...
DIAL 911.
TELL THEM YOU'VE FOUND A NINE-YEAR-OLD BOY WHO'S...
TRAPPED IN A COMIC BOO
© JULES FEIFFER
www.julesfeiffer.com

THIS IS THE WORST THING THAT EVER HAPPENED TO ANYBODY, ESPECIALLY ME, BECAUSE I DON'T EVEN READ COMIC BOOKS—

THAT MUCH. I MEAN, I READ THEM—WHY NOT?—BUT ALL THOSE SUPERHEROES FIGHTING SUPERVILLAINS WITH MUSCLES I COULDN'T HAVE IN A MILLION YEARS—

LIKE IF ONE OF THEM HIT ME EVEN ONCE BY ACCIDENT, I'D BE **BUG SPLATTER!**

AND THIS IS WHAT I'M EXPLAINING TO THIS CARTOONIST IN HIS STUDIO WHERE I'M ON A SCHOOL VISIT WITH MY CLASS:

SO I THINK IT WOULD BE BETTER IF YOU DREW SOMETHING REAL FOR A CHANGE, LIKE MY LITTLE BROTHER'S ALWAYS GETTING ME IN TROUBLE AND WHEN I PUSH HIM EVEN A LITTLE, WHOSE SIDE DOES MY MOTHER TAKE, EVEN WHEN HE STARTED IT? **HIS!** I MEAN, IF YOU DREW A COMIC ZAPPING A VILLAIN LIKE MY KID BROTHER, THAT'S A STORY KIDS LIKE ME WOULD GO OUT AND BUY.

I'M ONLY TRYING TO HELP HIM, BECAUSE NORMAL KIDS LIKE ME ARE THE ONES WHO READ HIS STUFF, SO SHOULDN'T HE WANT TO KNOW WHAT I THINK?

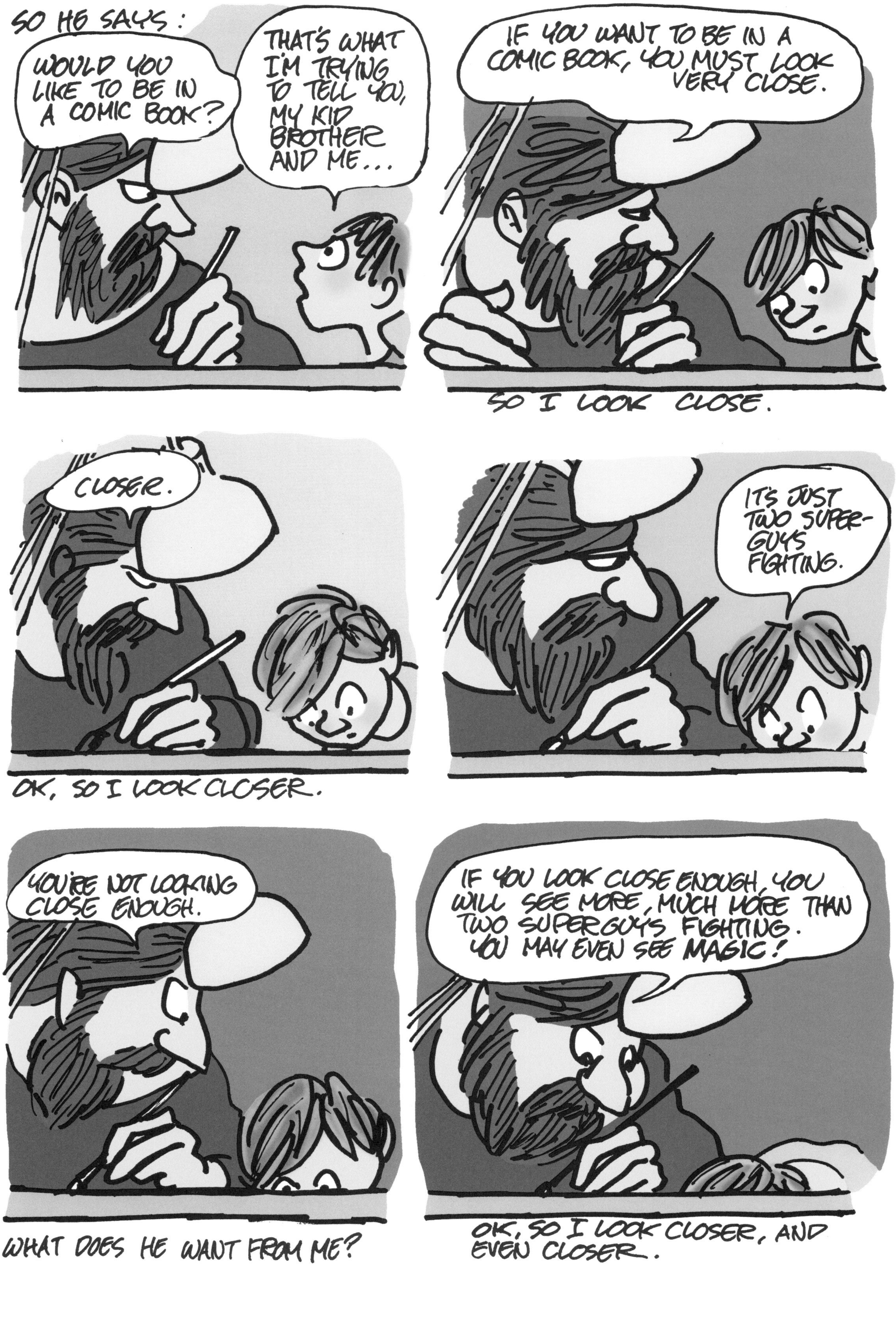
SO HE SAYS:
WOULD YOU LIKE TO BE IN A COMIC BOOK?
THAT'S WHAT I'M TRYING TO TELL YOU, MY KID BROTHER AND ME...
IF YOU WANT TO BE IN A COMIC BOOK, YOU MUST LOOK VERY CLOSE.
SO I LOOK CLOSE.
CLOSER.
OK, SO I LOOK CLOSER.
IT'S JUST TWO SUPER-GUYS FIGHTING.
YOU'RE NOT LOOKING CLOSE ENOUGH.
WHAT DOES HE WANT FROM ME?
IF YOU LOOK CLOSE ENOUGH, YOU WILL SEE MORE, MUCH MORE THAN TWO SUPERGUYS FIGHTING. YOU MAY EVEN SEE MAGIC!
OK, SO I LOOK CLOSER, AND EVEN CLOSER.

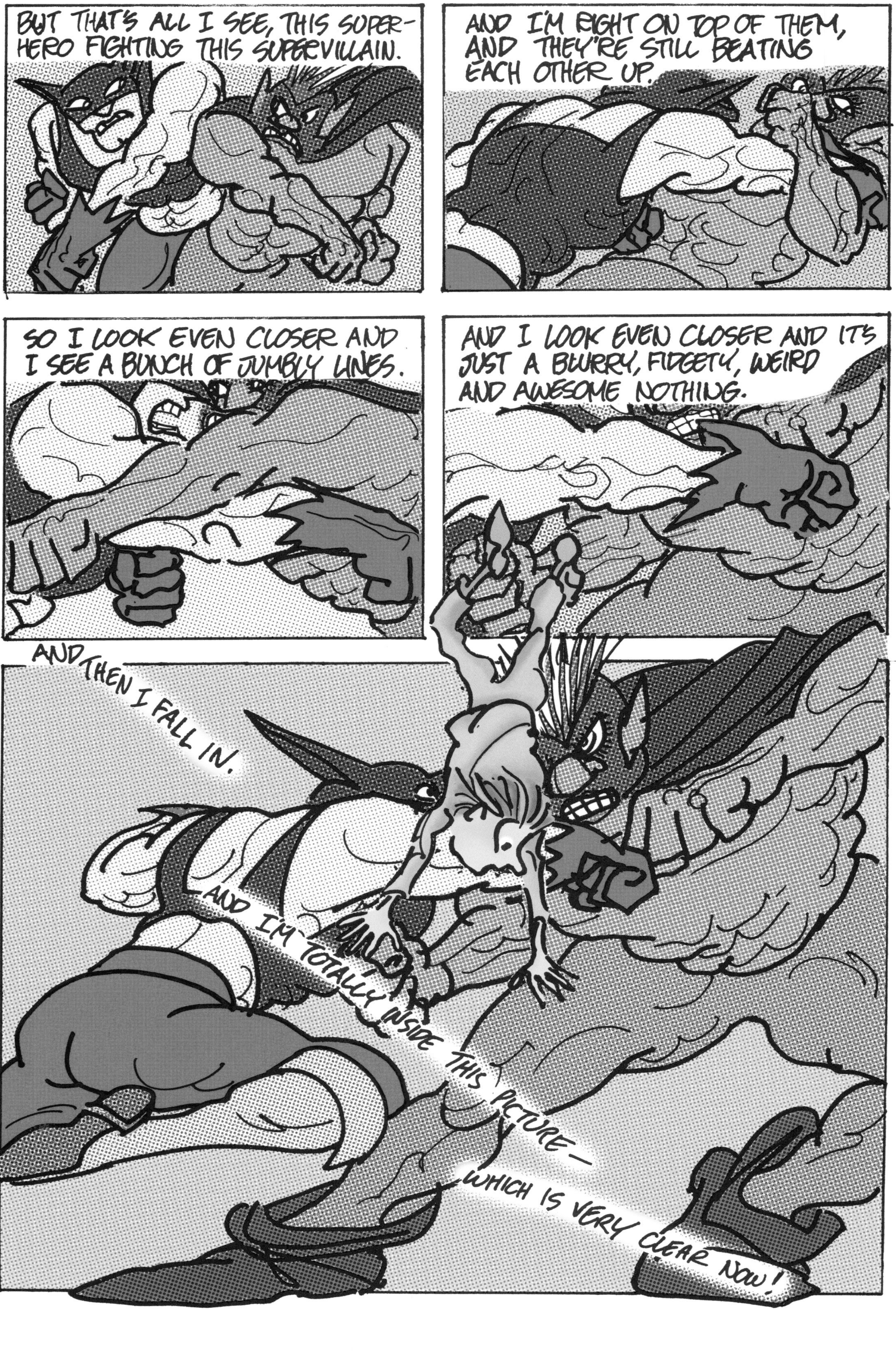
BUT THAT'S ALL I SEE, THIS SUPER-HERO FIGHTING THIS SUPERVILLAIN.
AND I'M RIGHT ON TOP OF THEM, AND THEY'RE STILL BEATING EACH OTHER UP.
SO I LOOK EVEN CLOSER AND I SEE A BUNCH OF JUMBLY LINES.
AND I LOOK EVEN CLOSER AND IT'S JUST A BLURRY, FIDGETY, WEIRD AND AWESOME NOTHING.
AND THEN I FALL IN.
AND I'M TOTALLY INSIDE THIS PICTURE—
WHICH IS VERY CLEAR NOW!

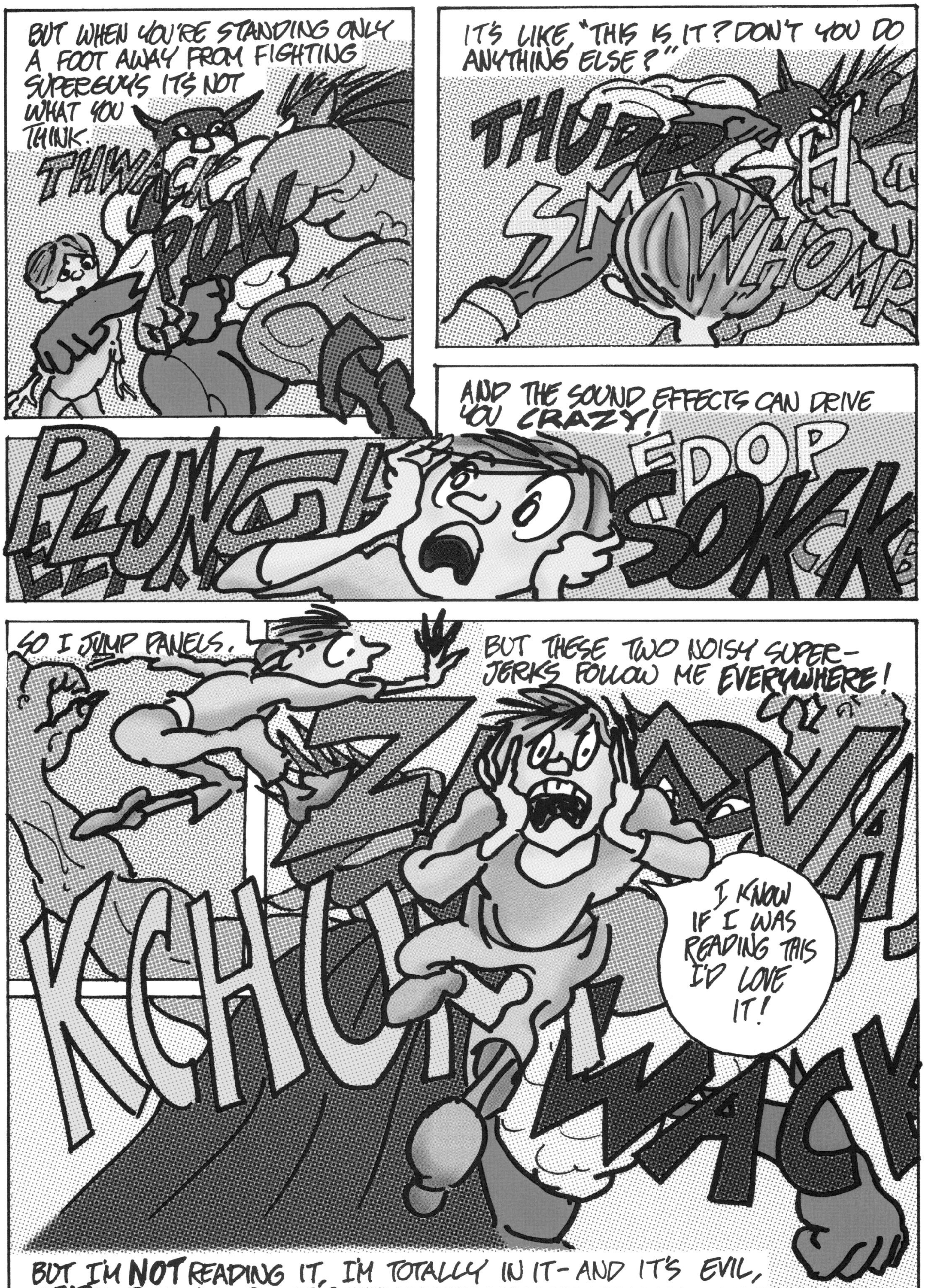
BUT WHEN YOU'RE STANDING ONLY A FOOT AWAY FROM FIGHTING SUPERGUYS IT'S NOT WHAT YOU THINK.
IT'S LIKE, "THIS IS IT? DON'T YOU DO ANYTHING ELSE?"
AND THE SOUND EFFECTS CAN DRIVE YOU CRAZY!
SO I JUMP PANELS.
BUT THESE TWO NOISY SUPER-JERKS FOLLOW ME EVERYWHERE!
I KNOW IF I WAS READING THIS I'D LOVE IT!
BUT I'M NOT READING IT, I'M TOTALLY IN IT- AND IT'S EVIL, STUPID, BORING PUKE!

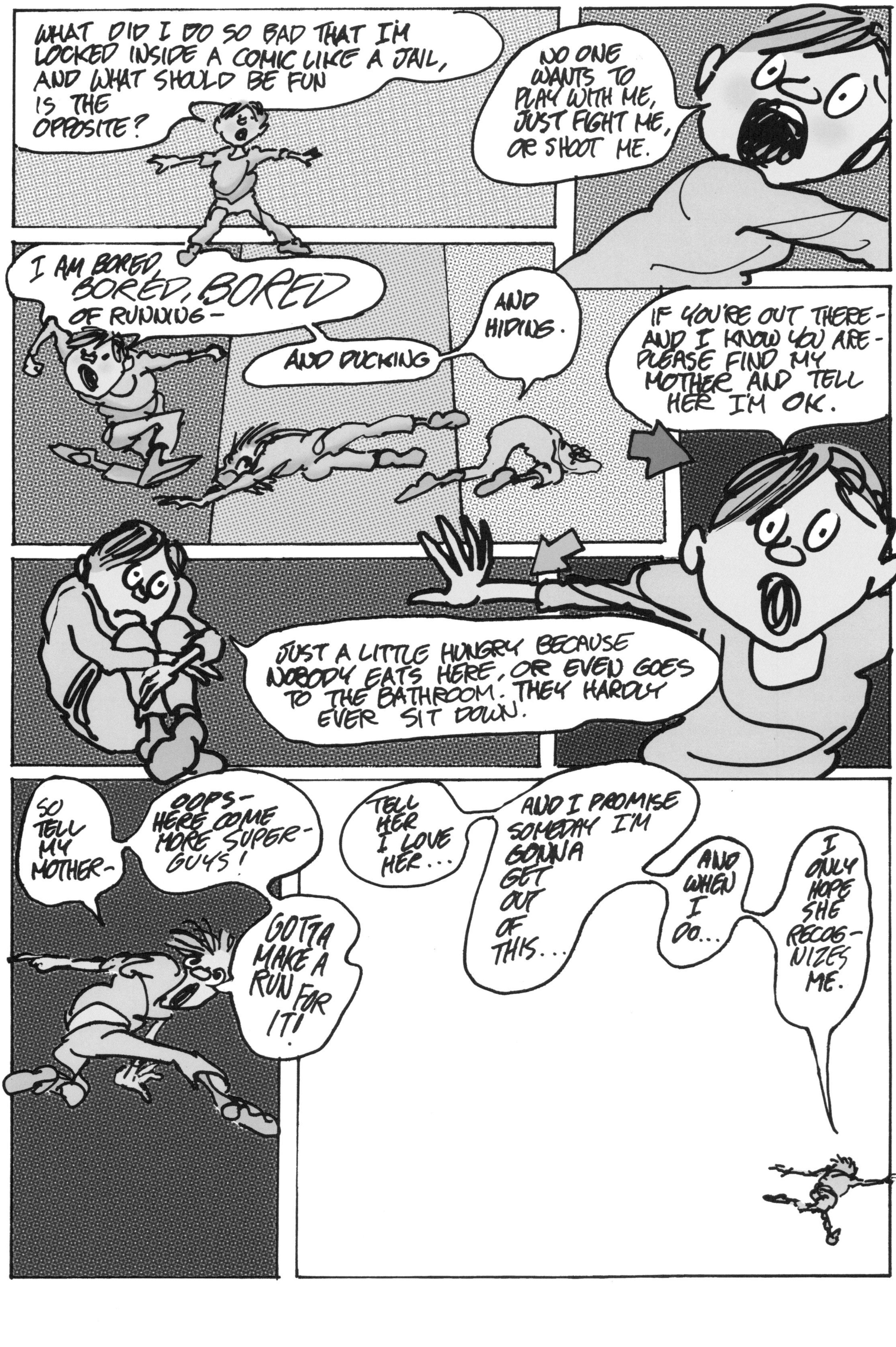
WHAT DID I DO SO BAD THAT I'M LOCKED INSIDE A COMIC LIKE A JAIL, AND WHAT SHOULD BE FUN IS THE OPPOSITE?
NO ONE WANTS TO PLAY WITH ME, JUST FIGHT ME, OR SHOOT ME.
I AM BORED, BORED, BORED OF RUNNING-
AND DUCKING
AND HIDING.
IF YOU'RE OUT THERE- AND I KNOW YOU ARE- PLEASE FIND MY MOTHER AND TELL HER I'M OK.
JUST A LITTLE HUNGRY BECAUSE NOBODY EATS HERE, OR EVEN GOES TO THE BATHROOM. THEY HARDLY EVER SIT DOWN.
SO TELL MY MOTHER-
OOPS- HERE COME MORE SUPER-GUYS!
GOTTA MAKE A RUN FOR IT!
TELL HER I LOVE HER...
AND I PROMISE SOMEDAY I'M GONNA GET OUT OF THIS...
AND WHEN I DO...
I ONLY HOPE SHE RECOGNIZES ME.

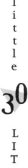

Mr. Frost

One nice spring morning the birds were singing, the bees were humming and Billy and I were swearing, because we had a math test...

And then the phone rang...

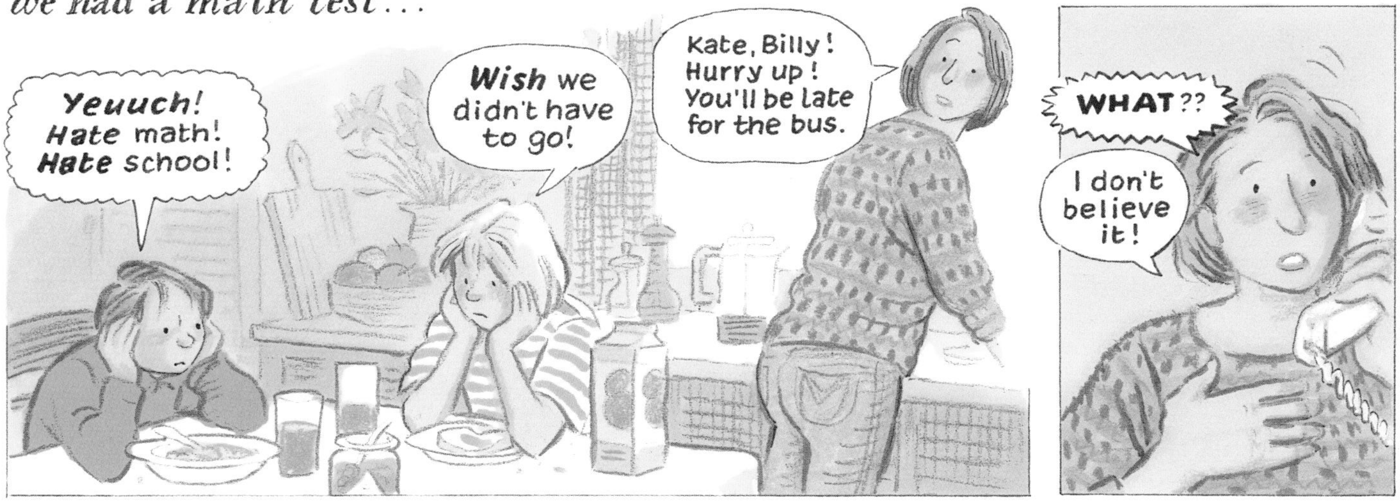
Yeuuch! Hate math! Hate school!
Wish we didn't have to go!
Kate, Billy! Hurry up! You'll be late for the bus.
WHAT??
I don't believe it!

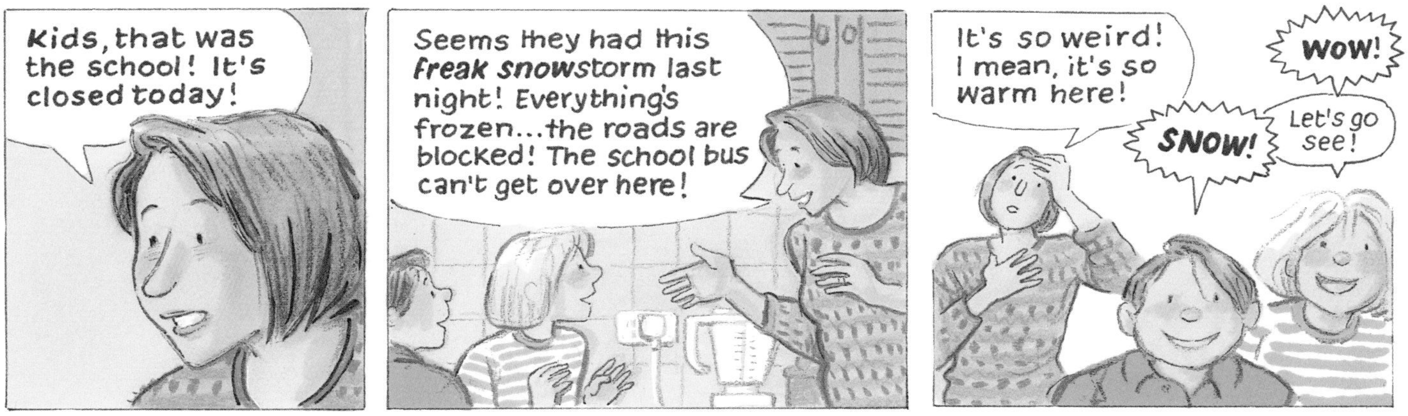
Kids, that was the school! It's closed today!
Seems they had this freak snowstorm last night! Everything's frozen...the roads are blocked! The school bus can't get over here!
It's so weird! I mean, it's so warm here!
SNOW!
WOW!
Let's go see!

We couldn't believe it...but it was true! Across the valley the hills and the roofs of Bellingham were covered in white.

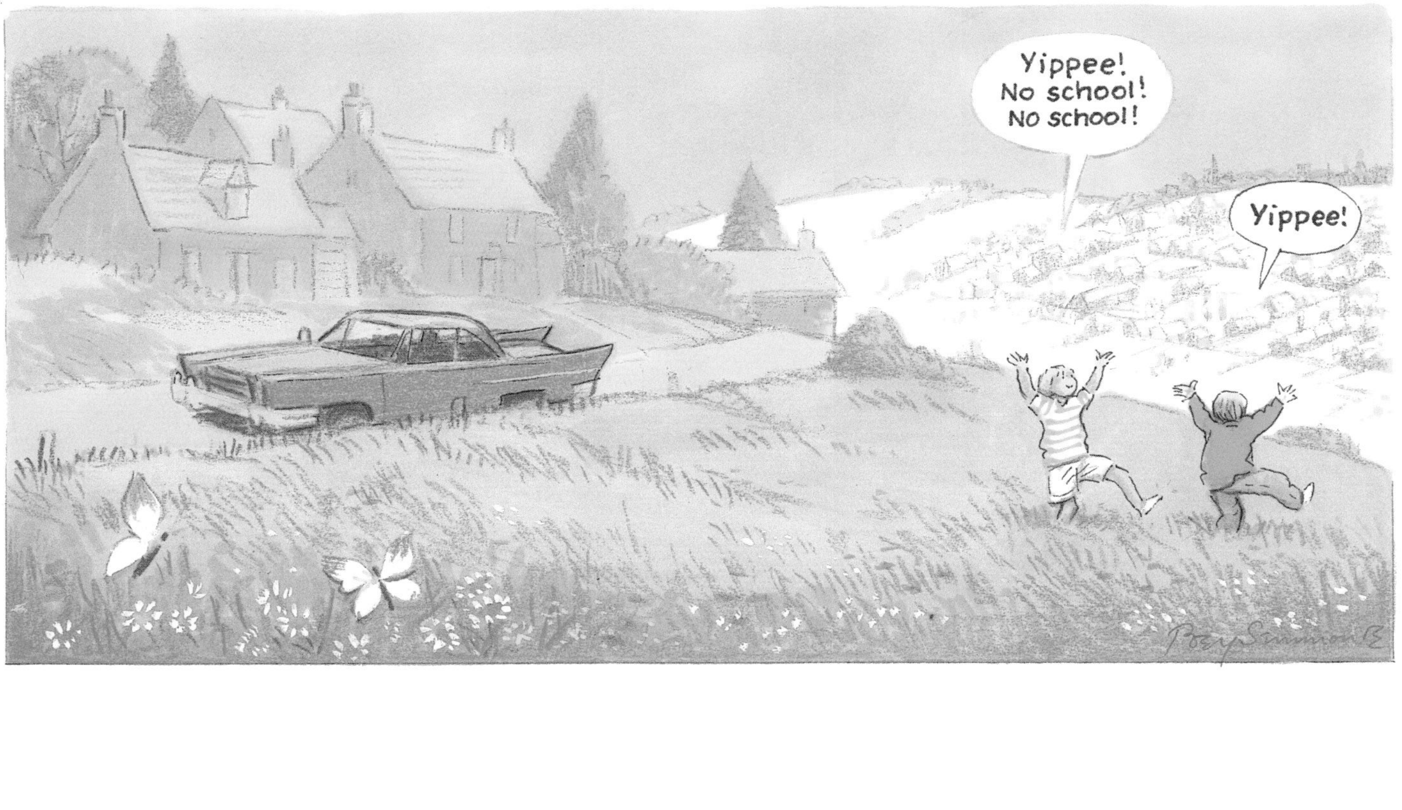
Yippee! No school! No school!
Yippee!

Just then, someone in this big old car began hooting and waving at us.

It was like a freezer door being opened. A blast of icy air came out of the car.

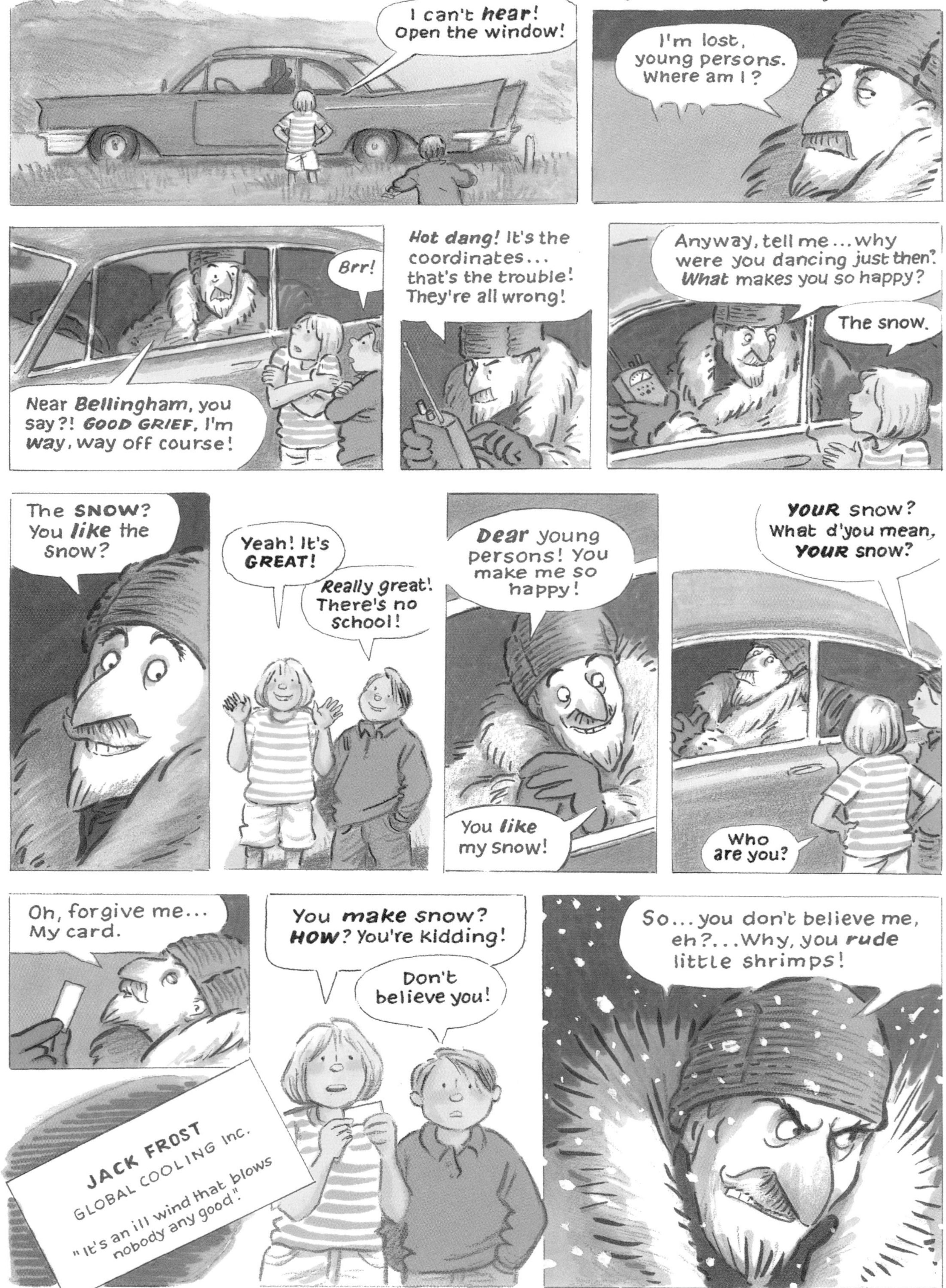
I can't **hear**! Open the window!
I'm lost, young persons. Where am I?
Brr!
Near **Bellingham**, you say?! **GOOD GRIEF**, I'm **way**, way off course!
Hot dang! It's the coordinates... that's the trouble! They're all wrong!
Anyway, tell me... why were you dancing just then? **What** makes you so happy?
The snow.
The **SNOW**? You **like** the snow?
Yeah! It's **GREAT**!
Really great! There's no school!
Dear young persons! You make me so happy!
You **like** my snow!
YOUR snow? What d'you mean, **YOUR** snow?
Who are you?
Oh, forgive me... My card.
JACK FROST
GLOBAL COOLING Inc.
"It's an ill wind that blows nobody any good"
You **make** snow? **HOW**? You're kidding!
Don't believe you!
So... you don't believe me, eh?... Why, you **rude** little shrimps!

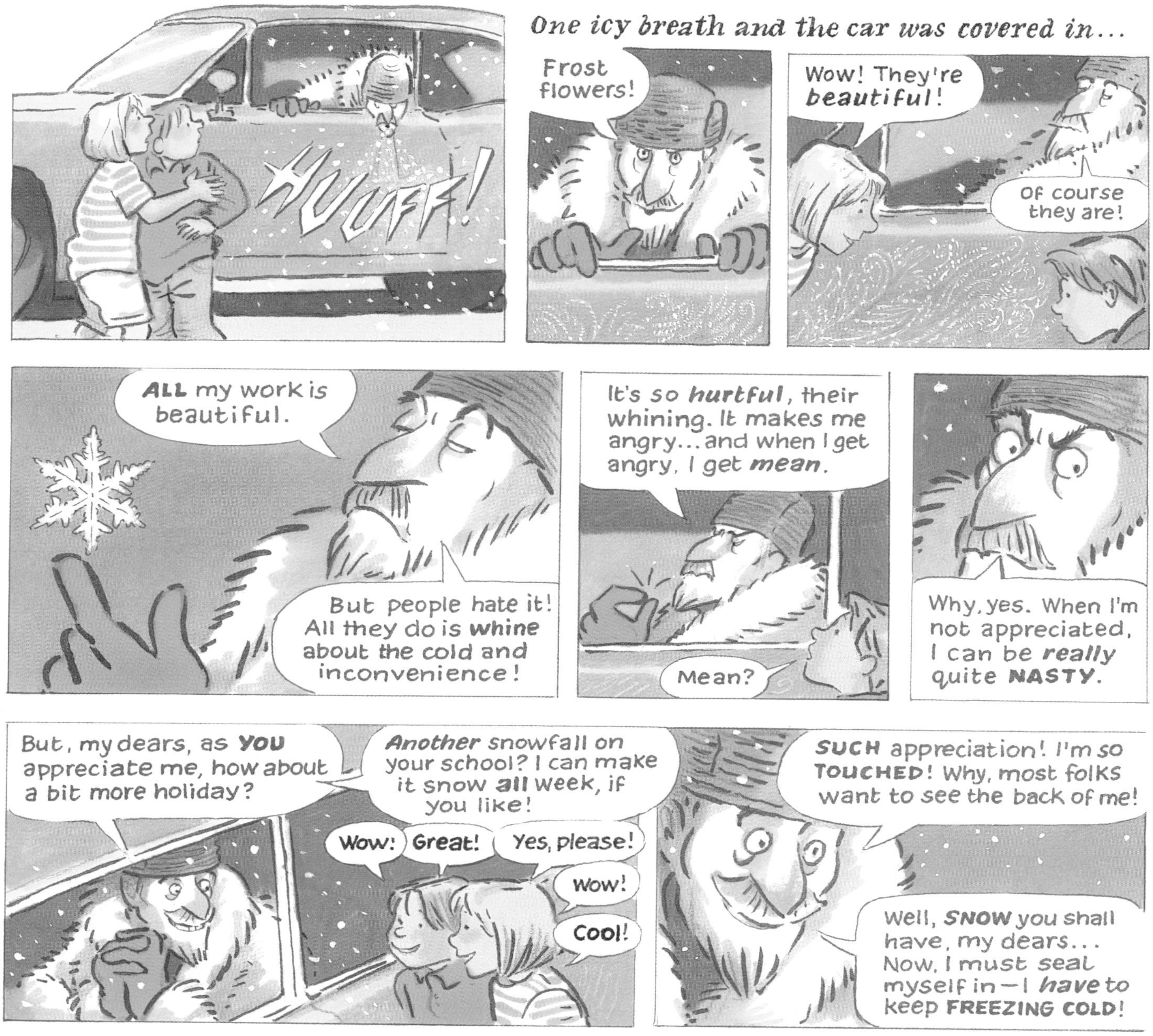
HUUFF!
One icy breath and the car was covered in...
Frost flowers!
Wow! They're **beautiful**!
Of course they are!
ALL my work is beautiful.
But people hate it! All they do is **whine** about the cold and inconvenience!
It's so **hurtful**, their whining. It makes me angry... and when I get angry, I get **mean**.
Mean?
Why, yes. When I'm not appreciated, I can be **really** quite **NASTY**.
But, my dears, as **YOU** appreciate me, how about a bit more holiday?
Another snowfall on your school? I can make it snow **all** week, if you like!
Wow!
Great!
Yes, please!
Wow!
Cool!
SUCH appreciation! I'm so **TOUCHED**! Why, most folks want to see the back of me!
Well, **SNOW** you shall have, my dears... Now, I must seal myself in—I **have** to keep **FREEZING COLD**!

Jack Frost parked in front of Mr. and Mrs. Woolley's house. How he knew that they were away on vacation, I don't know...but there he stayed, day after day.

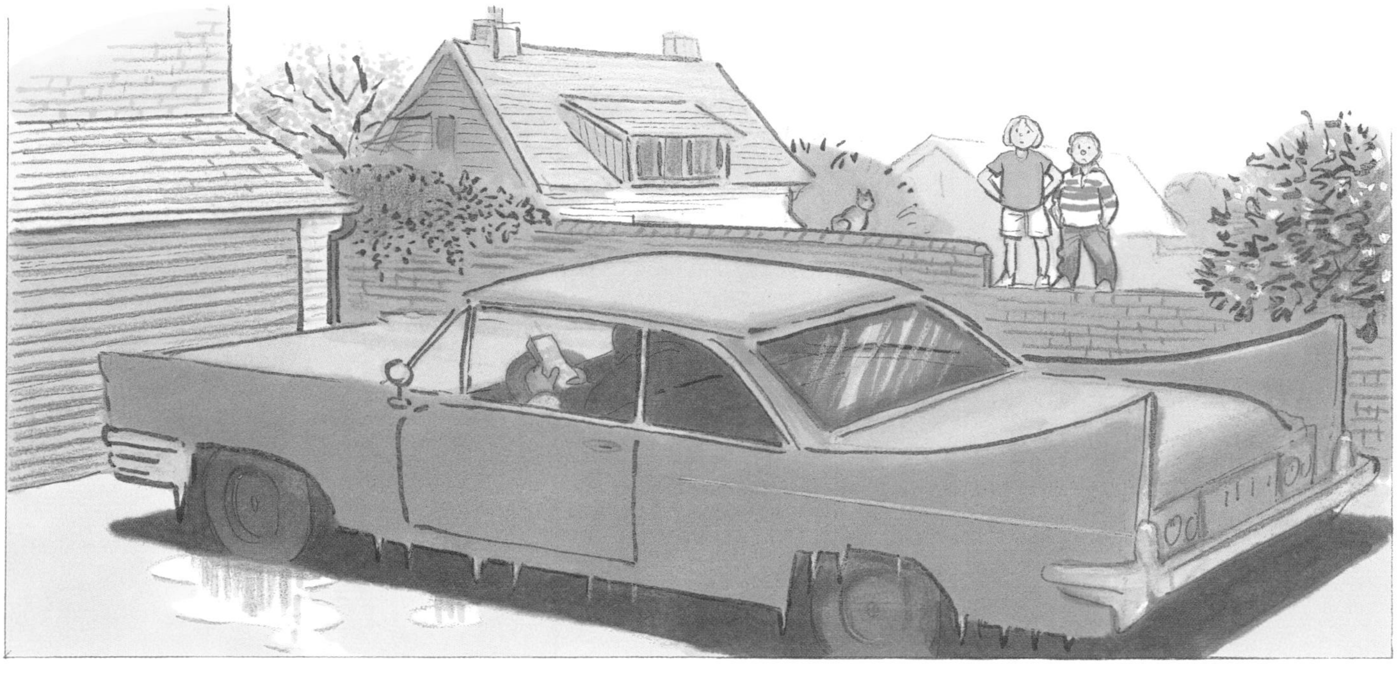

Every night it snowed across the valley around our school . . .

and every day Billy and I had a warm and sunny holiday.

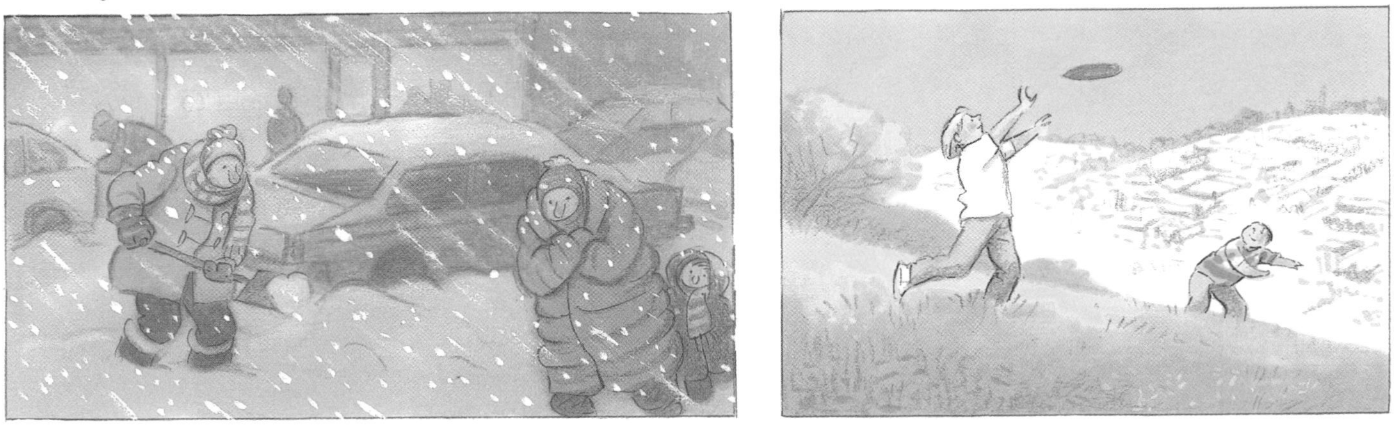

After three days we began to wish Mr. Frost would stop. We got bored, we missed our friends, we even missed school. And then, on the fourth day, we watched the news . . .

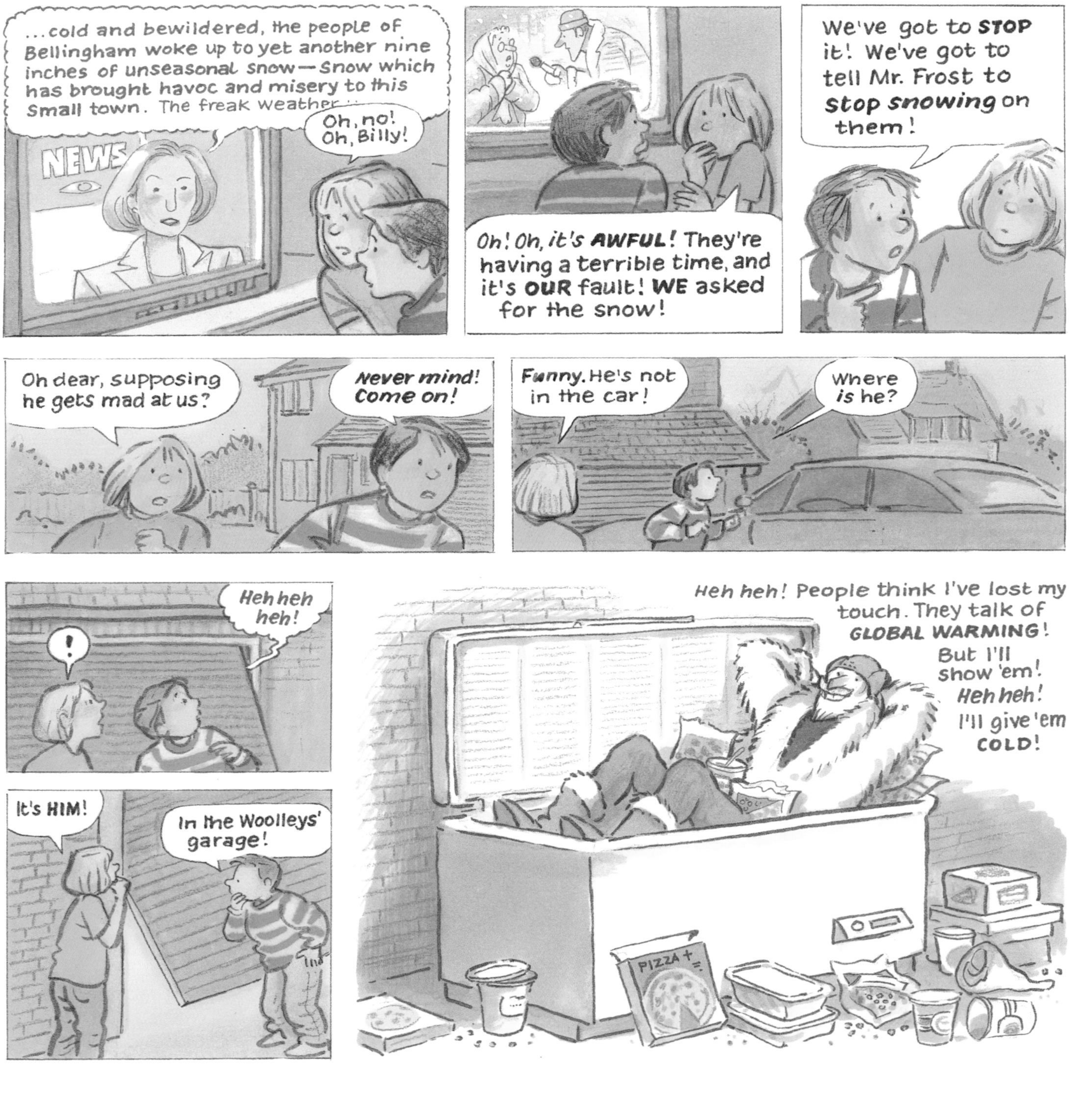

. . . cold and bewildered, the people of Bellingham woke up to yet another nine inches of unseasonal snow — snow which has brought havoc and misery to this small town. The freak weather
NEWS
Oh, no! Oh, Billy!
Oh! Oh, it's AWFUL! They're having a terrible time, and it's OUR fault! WE asked for the snow!
We've got to STOP it! We've got to tell Mr. Frost to stop snowing on them!
Oh dear, supposing he gets mad at us?
Never mind! Come on!
Funny. He's not in the car!
Where is he?
Heh heh heh!
!
It's HIM!
In the Woolleys' garage!
Heh heh! People think I've lost my touch. They talk of GLOBAL WARMING! But I'll show 'em! Heh heh! I'll give 'em COLD!
PIZZA

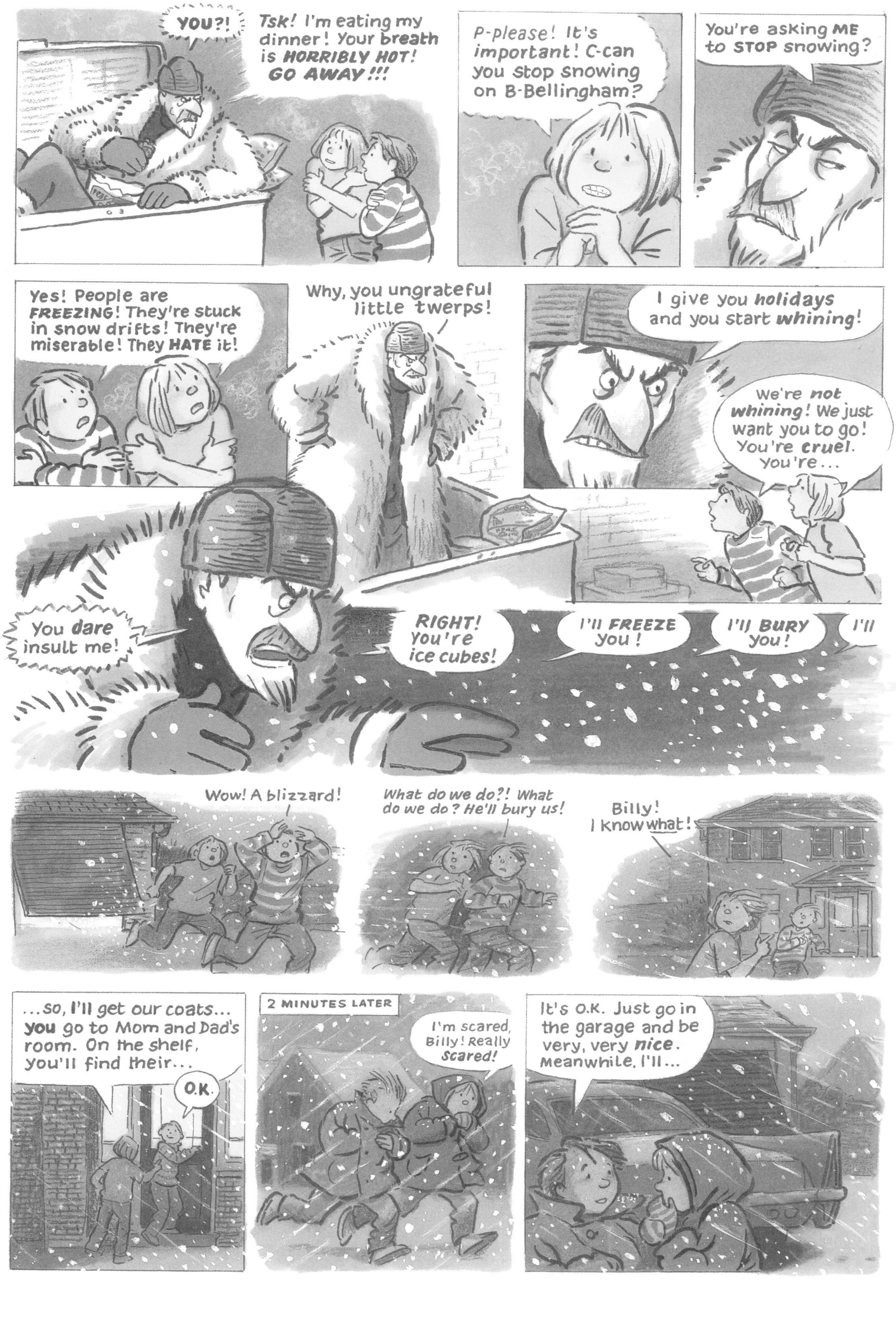
YOU?!
Tsk! I'm eating my dinner! Your breath is HORRIBLY HOT! GO AWAY!!!
P-please! It's important! C-can you stop snowing on B-Bellingham?
You're asking ME to STOP snowing?
Yes! People are FREEZING! They're stuck in snow drifts! They're miserable! They HATE it!
Why, you ungrateful little twerps!
I give you holidays and you start whining!
We're not whining! We just want you to go! You're cruel. You're...
You dare insult me!
RIGHT! You're ice cubes!
I'll FREEZE you!
I'll BURY you!
I'll
Wow! A blizzard!
What do we do?! What do we do? He'll bury us!
Billy! I know what!
...so, I'll get our coats... you go to Mom and Dad's room. On the shelf, you'll find their...
O.K.
2 MINUTES LATER
I'm scared, Billy! Really scared!
It's O.K. Just go in the garage and be very, very nice. Meanwhile, I'll...

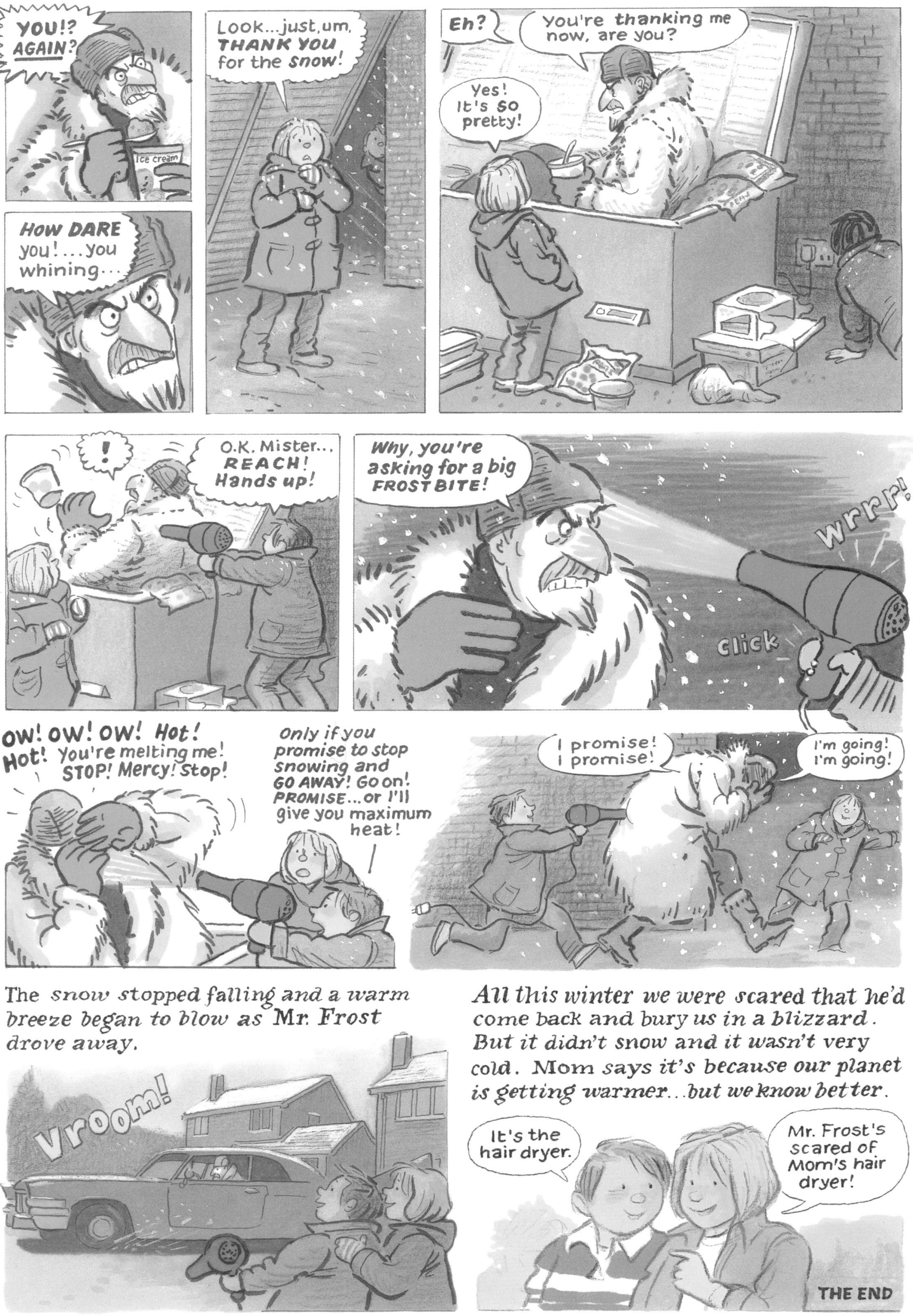
YOU!? AGAIN?
Ice cream
HOW DARE you!...you whining...
Look...just, um, THANK YOU for the snow!
Eh?
You're thanking me now, are you?
Yes! It's so pretty!
!
O.K. Mister... REACH! Hands up!
Why, you're asking for a big FROST BITE!
wrrr!
click
OW! OW! OW! Hot! Hot! You're melting me! STOP! Mercy! Stop!
Only if you promise to stop snowing and GO AWAY! Go on! PROMISE...or I'll give you maximum heat!
I promise! I promise!
I'm going! I'm going!
The snow stopped falling and a warm breeze began to blow as Mr. Frost drove away.
Vroom!
All this winter we were scared that he'd come back and bury us in a blizzard. But it didn't snow and it wasn't very cold. Mom says it's because our planet is getting warmer...but we know better.
It's the hair dryer.
Mr. Frost's scared of Mom's hair dryer!
THE END

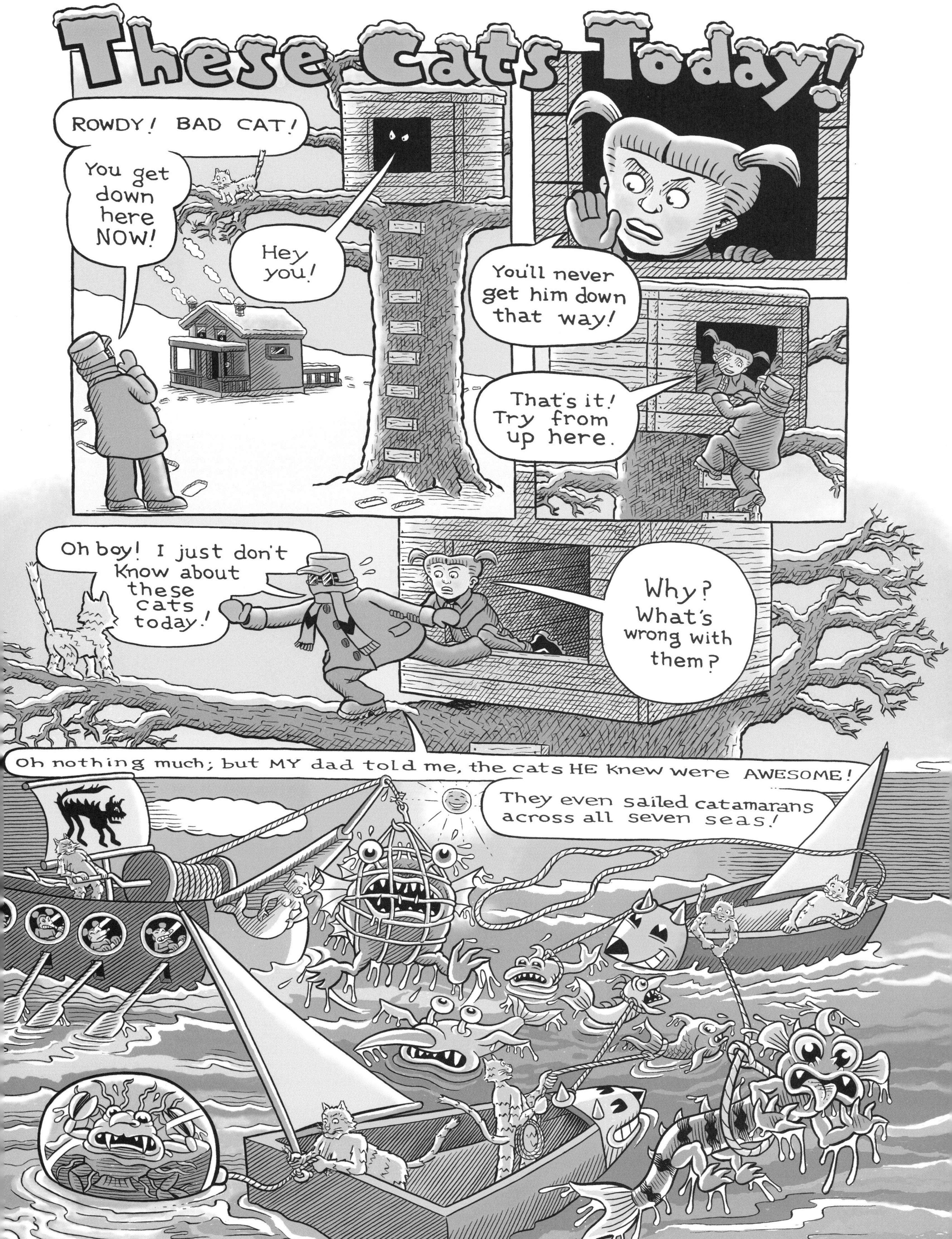
These Cats Today!
ROWDY! BAD CAT!
You get down here NOW!
Hey you!
You'll never get him down that way!
That's it! Try from up here.
Oh boy! I just don't know about these cats today!
Why? What's wrong with them?
Oh nothing much; but MY dad told me, the cats HE knew were AWESOME!
They even sailed catamarans across all seven seas!

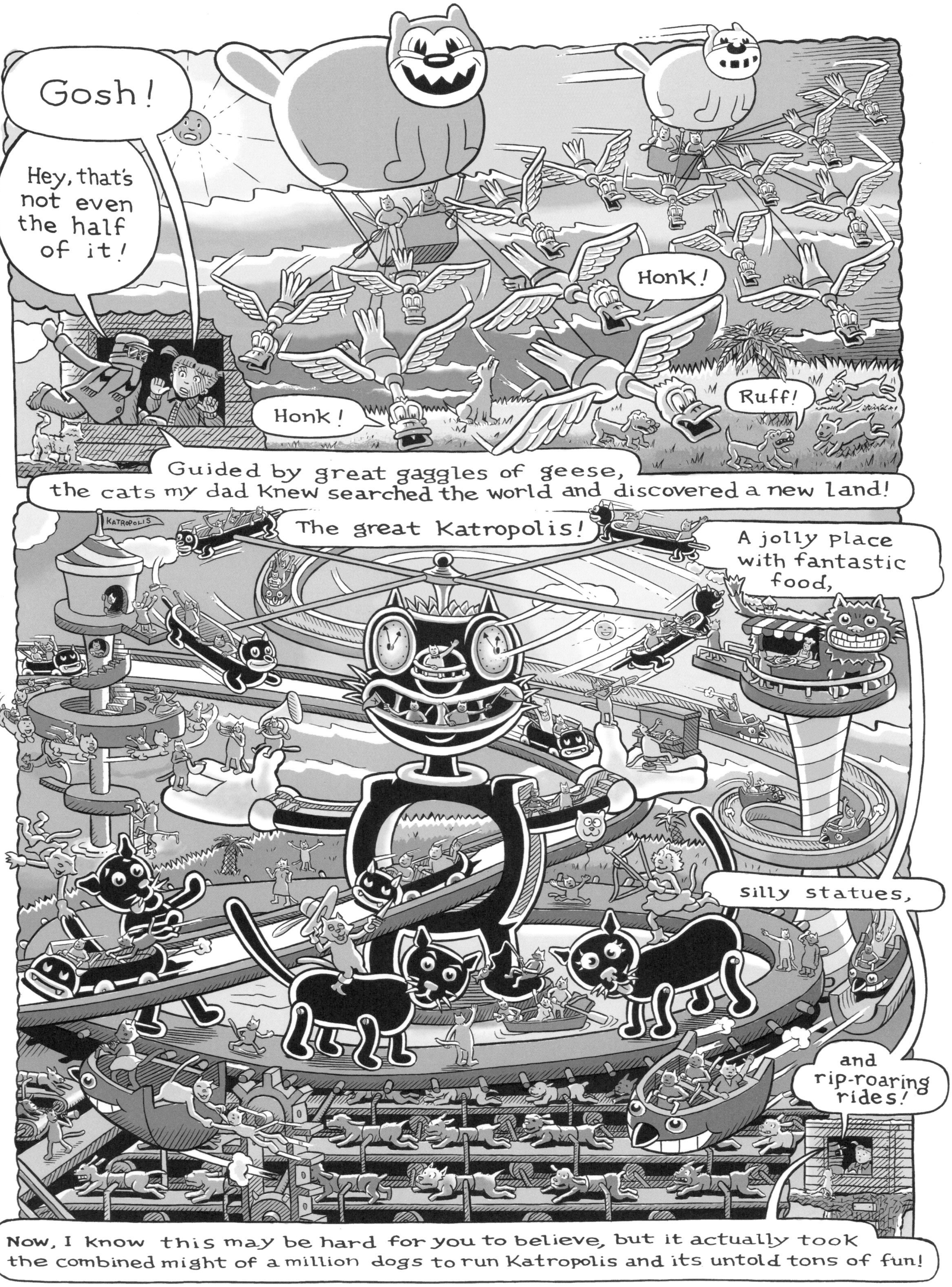
Gosh!
Hey, that's not even the half of it!
Honk!
Honk!
Ruff!
Guided by great gaggles of geese, the cats my dad knew searched the world and discovered a new land!
KATROPOLIS
The great Katropolis!
A jolly place with fantastic food,
silly statues,
and rip-roaring rides!
Now, I know this may be hard for you to believe, but it actually took the combined might of a million dogs to run Katropolis and its untold tons of fun!

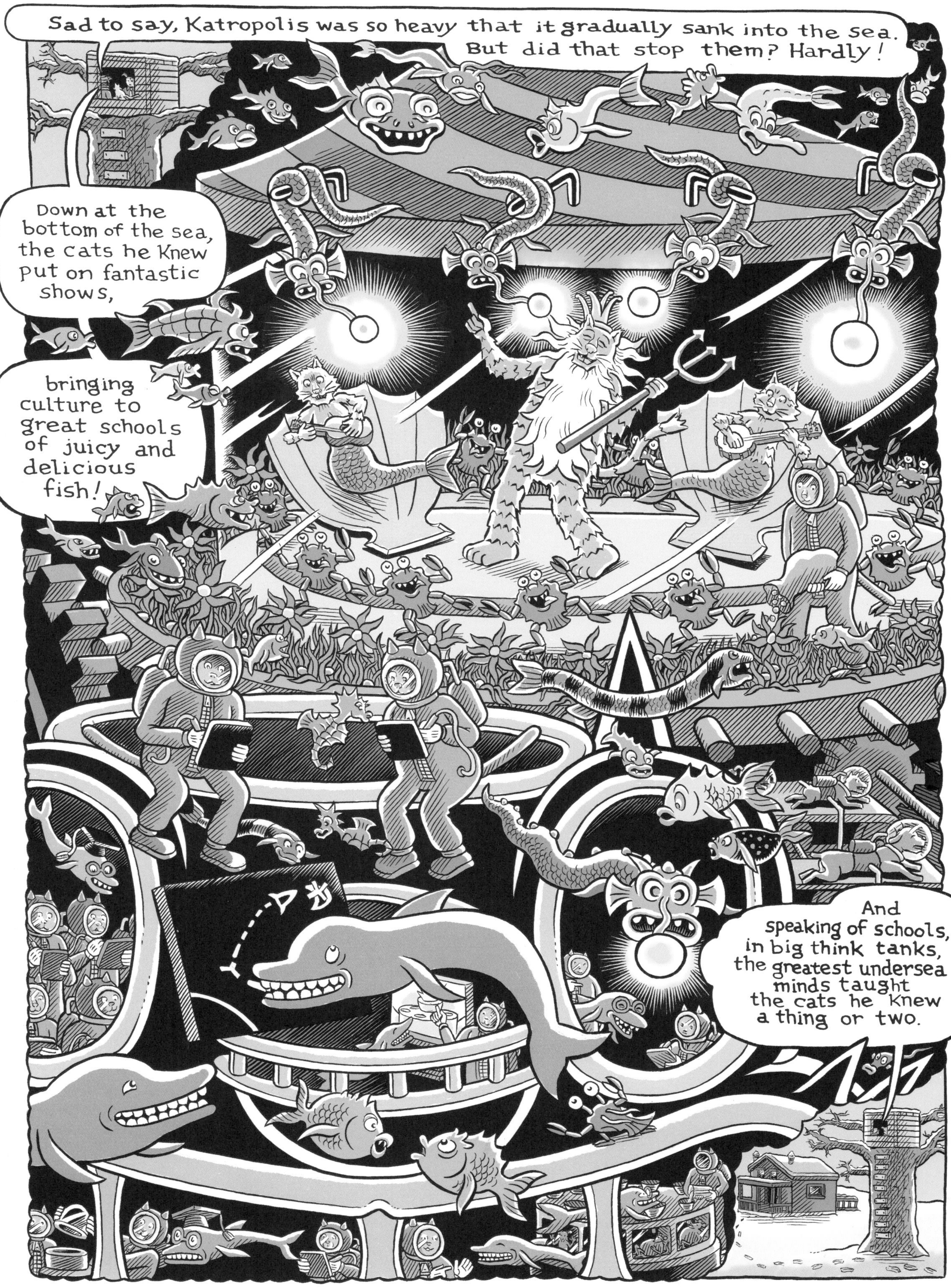
Sad to say, Katropolis was so heavy that it gradually sank into the sea. But did that stop them? Hardly!
Down at the bottom of the sea, the cats he knew put on fantastic shows,
bringing culture to great schools of juicy and delicious fish!
And speaking of schools, in big think tanks, the greatest undersea minds taught the cats he knew a thing or two.

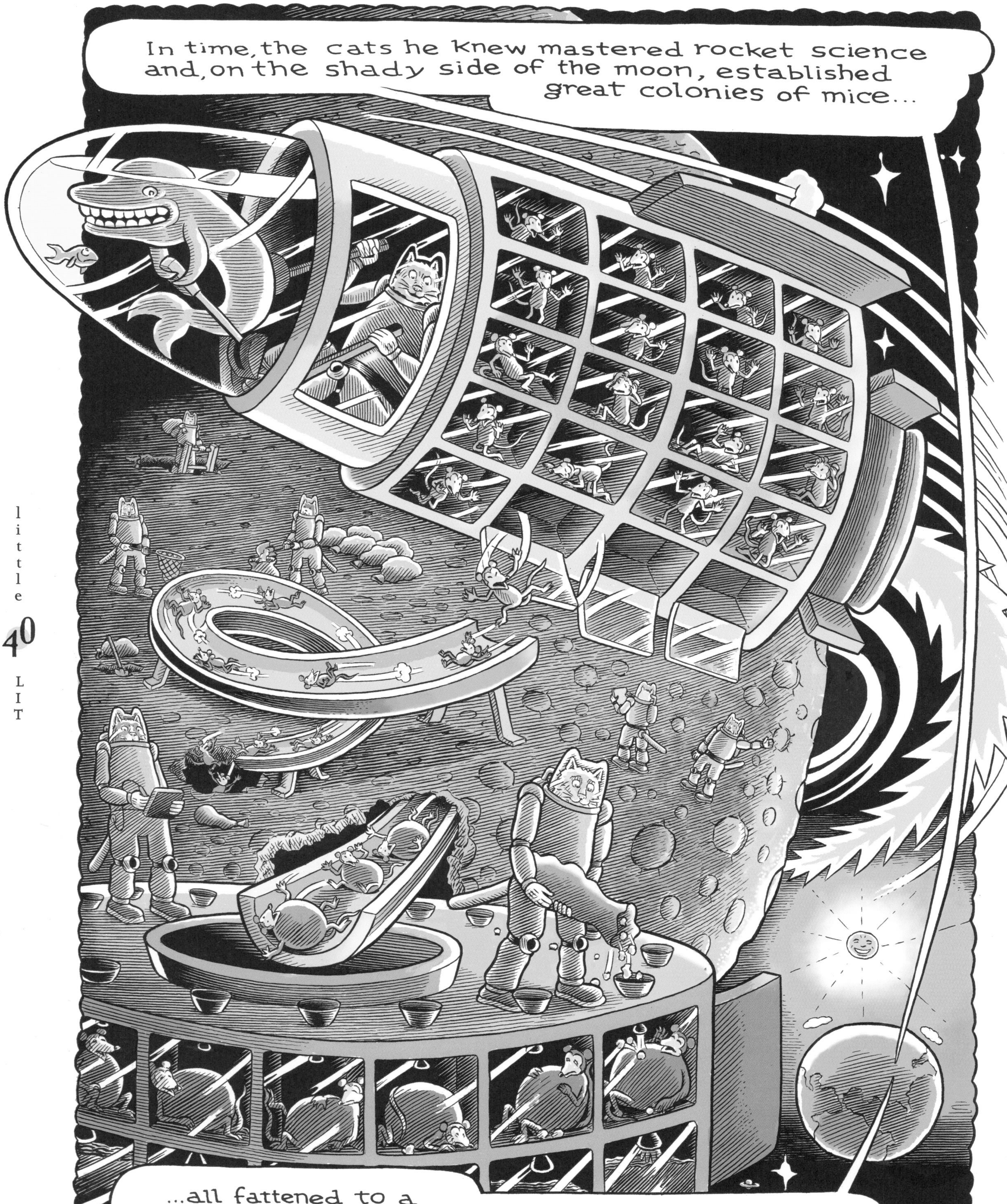
In time, the cats he knew mastered rocket science and, on the shady side of the moon, established great colonies of mice...
...all fattened to a fare-thee-well on good green cheese!

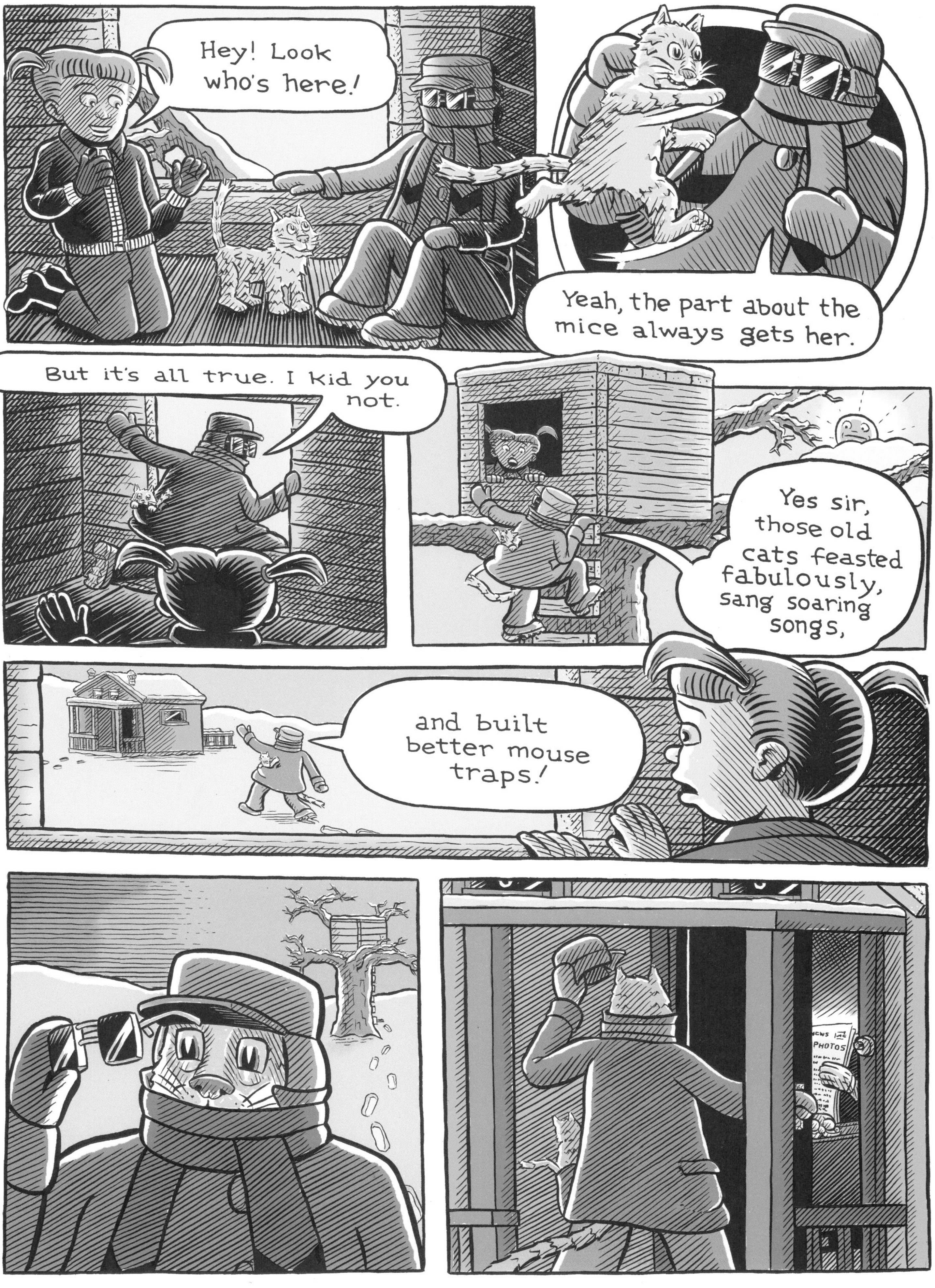
Hey! Look who's here!
Yeah, the part about the mice always gets her.
But it's all true. I kid you not.
Yes sir, those old cats feasted fabulously, sang soaring songs,
and built better mouse traps!

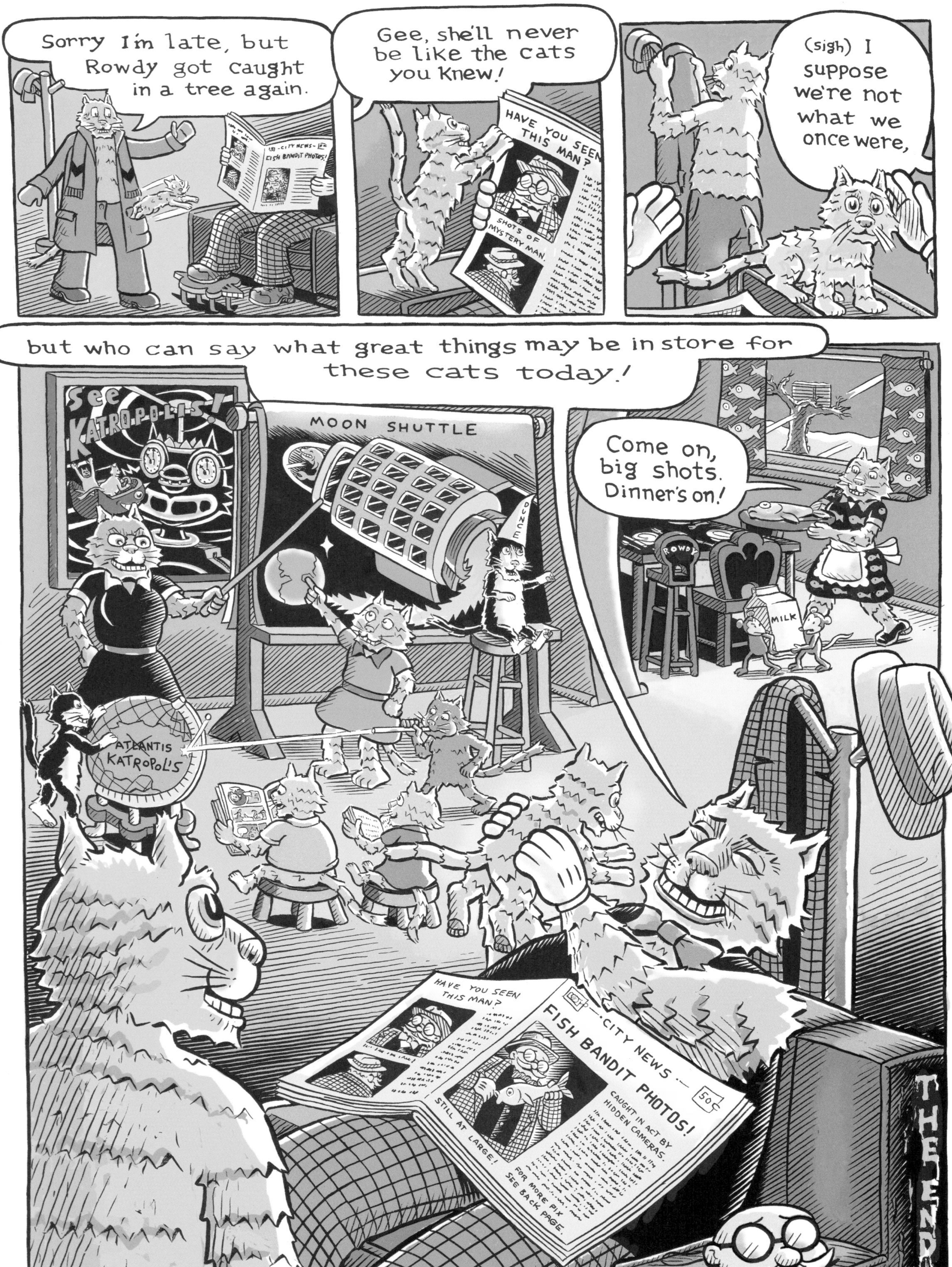
Sorry I'm late, but Rowdy got caught in a tree again.
Gee, she'll never be like the cats you knew!
HAVE YOU SEEN THIS MAN?
SHOTS OF MYSTERY MAN.
(sigh) I suppose we're not what we once were,
but who can say what great things may be in store for these cats today!
See KATROPOLIS!
MOON SHUTTLE
DUNCE
ATLANTIS KATROPOLIS
Come on, big shots. Dinner's on!
ROWDY
MILK
HAVE YOU SEEN THIS MAN?
CITY NEWS
50¢
FISH BANDIT PHOTOS!
CAUGHT IN ACT BY HIDDEN CAMERAS.
STILL AT LARGE!
FOR MORE PIX SEE BACK PAGE.
THE END

Kim Deitch

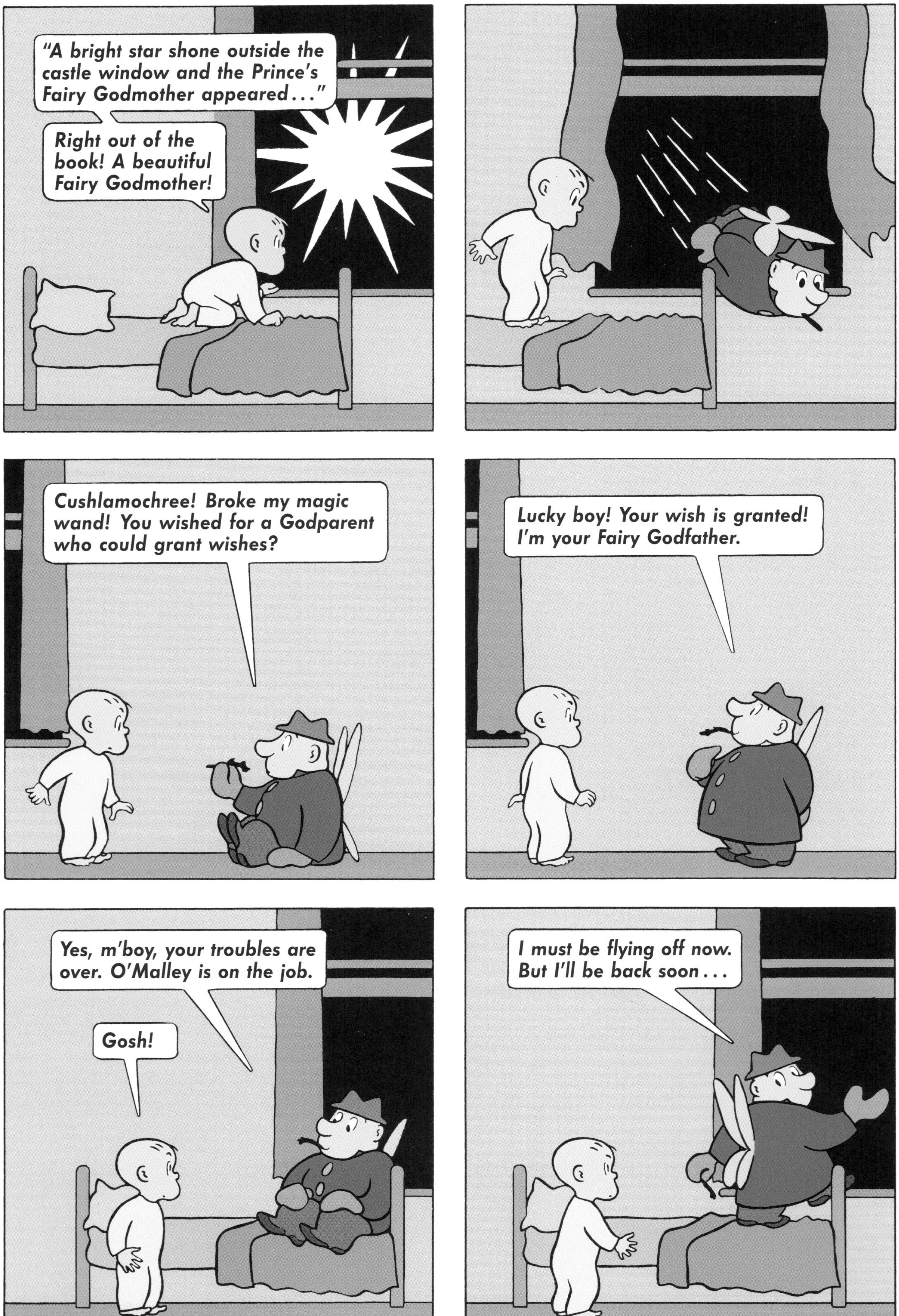

"A bright star shone outside the castle window and the Prince's Fairy Godmother appeared..."
Right out of the book! A beautiful Fairy Godmother!
Cushlamochree! Broke my magic wand! You wished for a Godparent who could grant wishes?
Lucky boy! Your wish is granted! I'm your Fairy Godfather.
Yes, m'boy, your troubles are over. O'Malley is on the job.
Gosh!
I must be flying off now. But I'll be back soon...

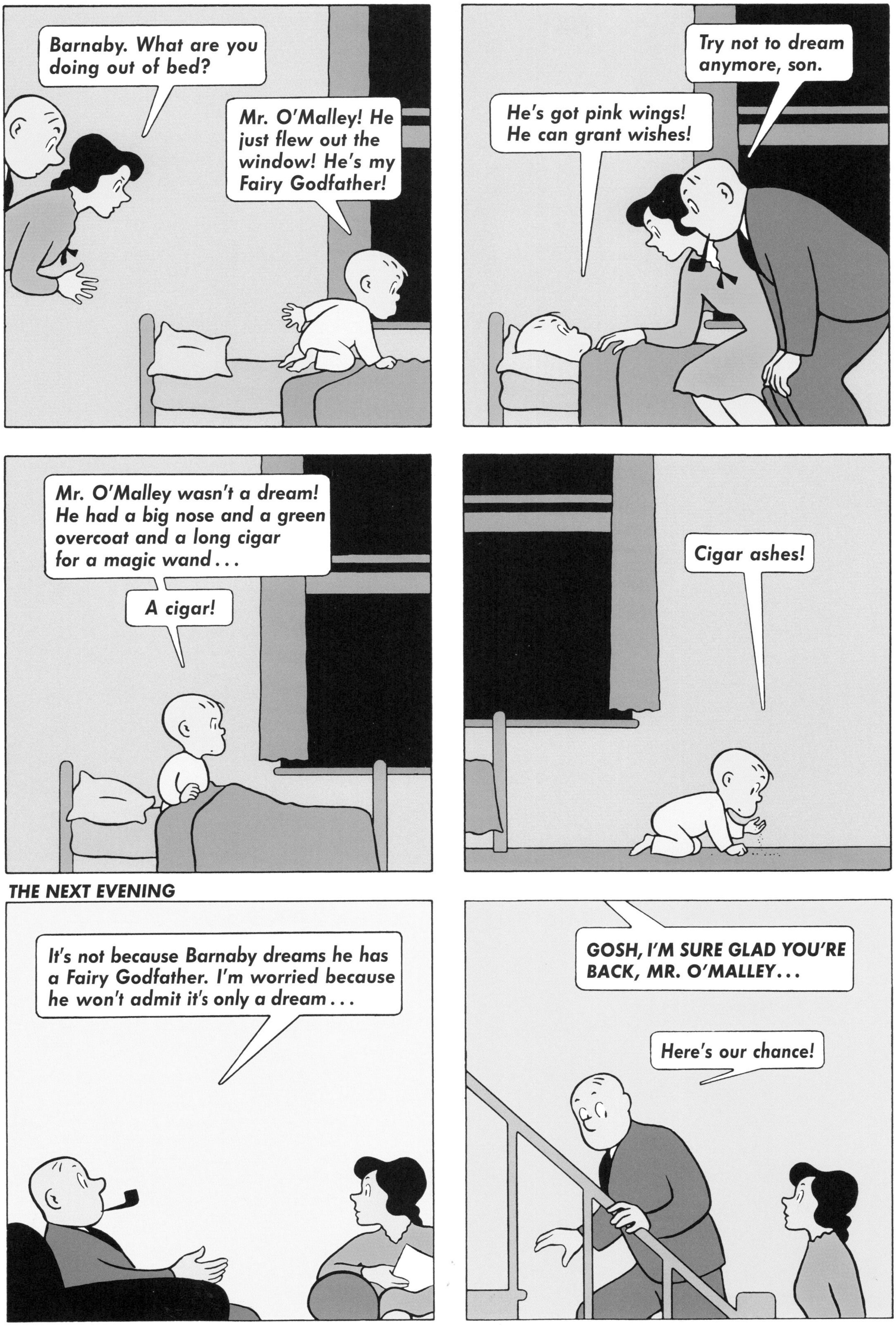
Barnaby. What are you doing out of bed?
Mr. O'Malley! He just flew out the window! He's my Fairy Godfather!
He's got pink wings! He can grant wishes!
Try not to dream anymore, son.
Mr. O'Malley wasn't a dream! He had a big nose and a green overcoat and a long cigar for a magic wand...
A cigar!
Cigar ashes!
THE NEXT EVENING
It's not because Barnaby dreams he has a Fairy Godfather. I'm worried because he won't admit it's only a dream...
GOSH, I'M SURE GLAD YOU'RE BACK, MR. O'MALLEY...
Here's our chance!

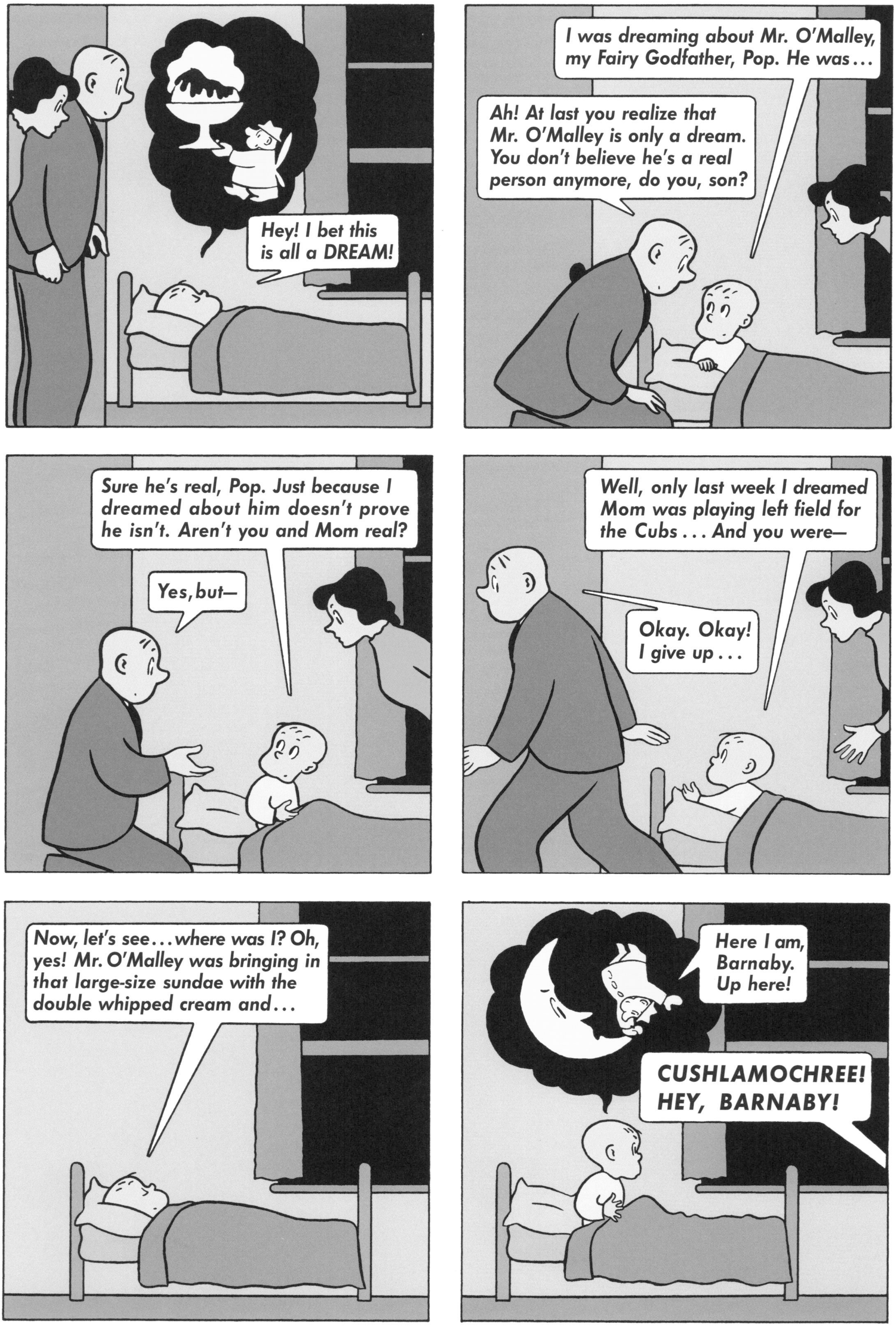
Hey! I bet this is all a DREAM!
I was dreaming about Mr. O'Malley, my Fairy Godfather, Pop. He was...
Ah! At last you realize that Mr. O'Malley is only a dream. You don't believe he's a real person anymore, do you, son?
Sure he's real, Pop. Just because I dreamed about him doesn't prove he isn't. Aren't you and Mom real?
Yes, but—
Well, only last week I dreamed Mom was playing left field for the Cubs... And you were—
Okay. Okay! I give up...
Now, let's see...where was I? Oh, yes! Mr. O'Malley was bringing in that large-size sundae with the double whipped cream and...
Here I am, Barnaby. Up here!
CUSHLAMOCHREE! HEY, BARNABY!

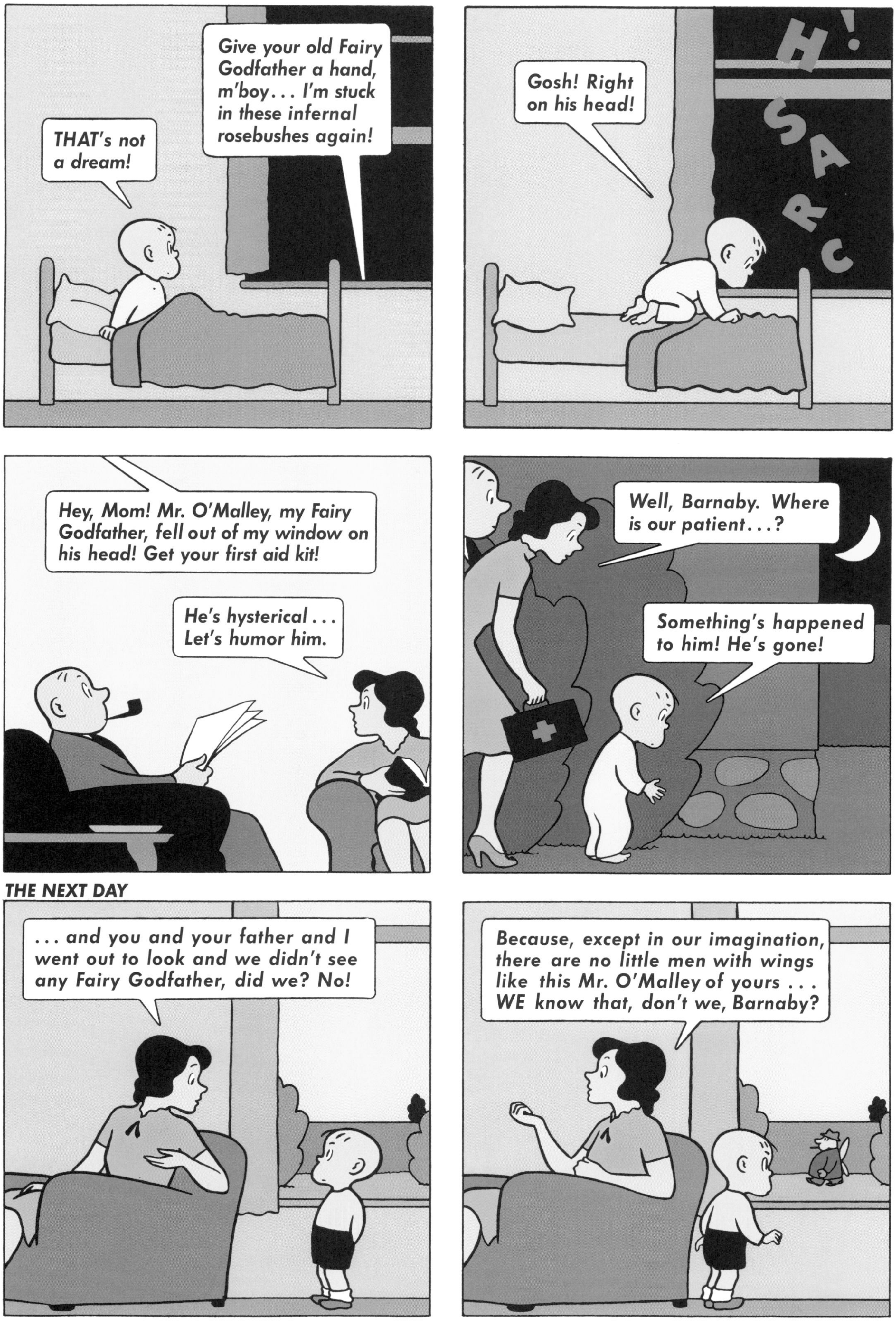
THAT's not a dream!
Give your old Fairy Godfather a hand, m'boy... I'm stuck in these infernal rosebushes again!
Gosh! Right on his head!
CRASH!
Hey, Mom! Mr. O'Malley, my Fairy Godfather, fell out of my window on his head! Get your first aid kit!
He's hysterical... Let's humor him.
Well, Barnaby. Where is our patient...?
Something's happened to him! He's gone!
THE NEXT DAY
... and you and your father and I went out to look and we didn't see any Fairy Godfather, did we? No!
Because, except in our imagination, there are no little men with wings like this Mr. O'Malley of yours... WE know that, don't we, Barnaby?

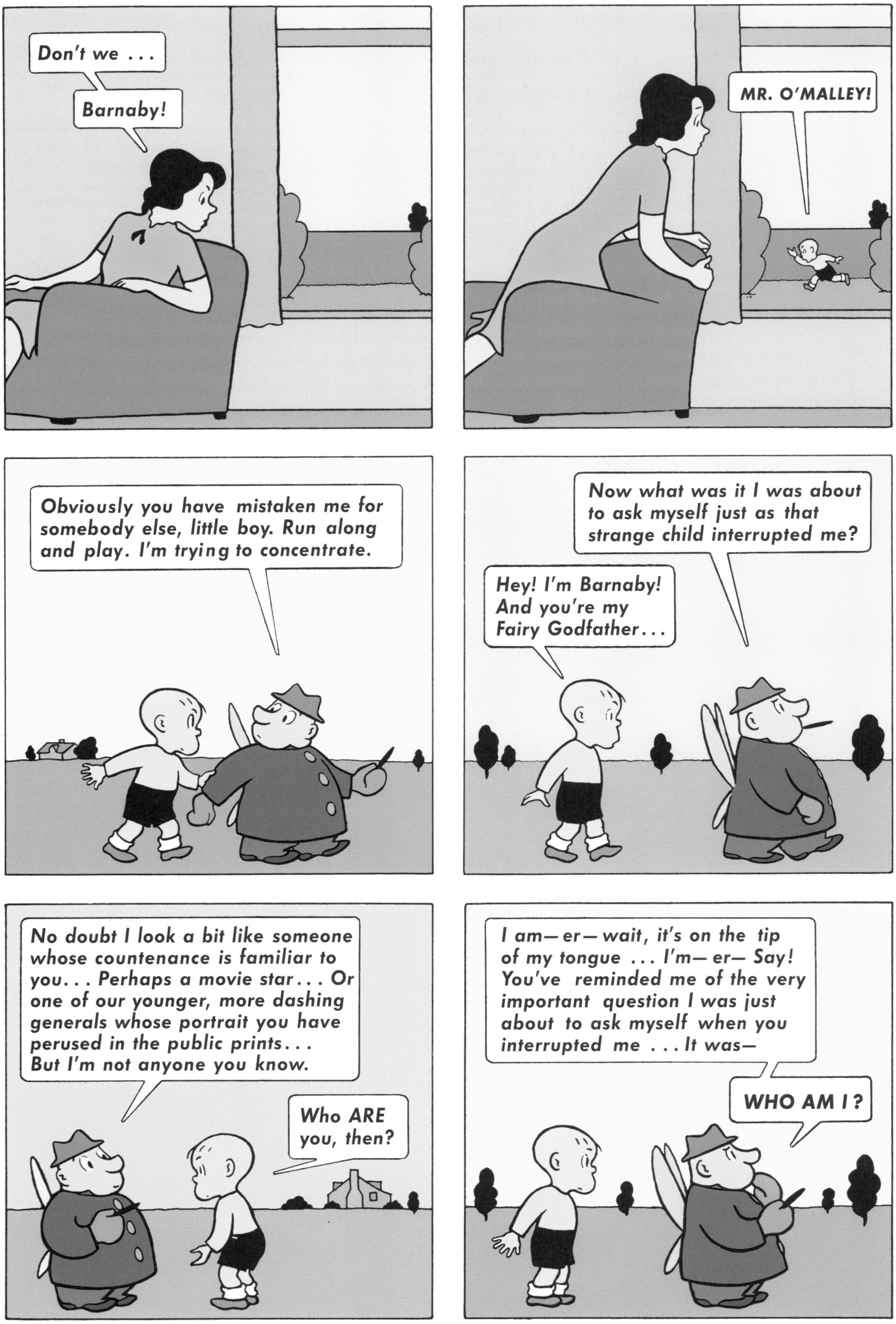
Don't we . . .
Barnaby!
MR. O'MALLEY!
Obviously you have mistaken me for somebody else, little boy. Run along and play. I'm trying to concentrate.
Now what was it I was about to ask myself just as that strange child interrupted me?
Hey! I'm Barnaby! And you're my Fairy Godfather...
No doubt I look a bit like someone whose countenance is familiar to you... Perhaps a movie star... Or one of our younger, more dashing generals whose portrait you have perused in the public prints... But I'm not anyone you know.
Who ARE you, then?
I am—er—wait, it's on the tip of my tongue ... I'm—er— Say! You've reminded me of the very important question I was just about to ask myself when you interrupted me ... It was—
WHO AM I?

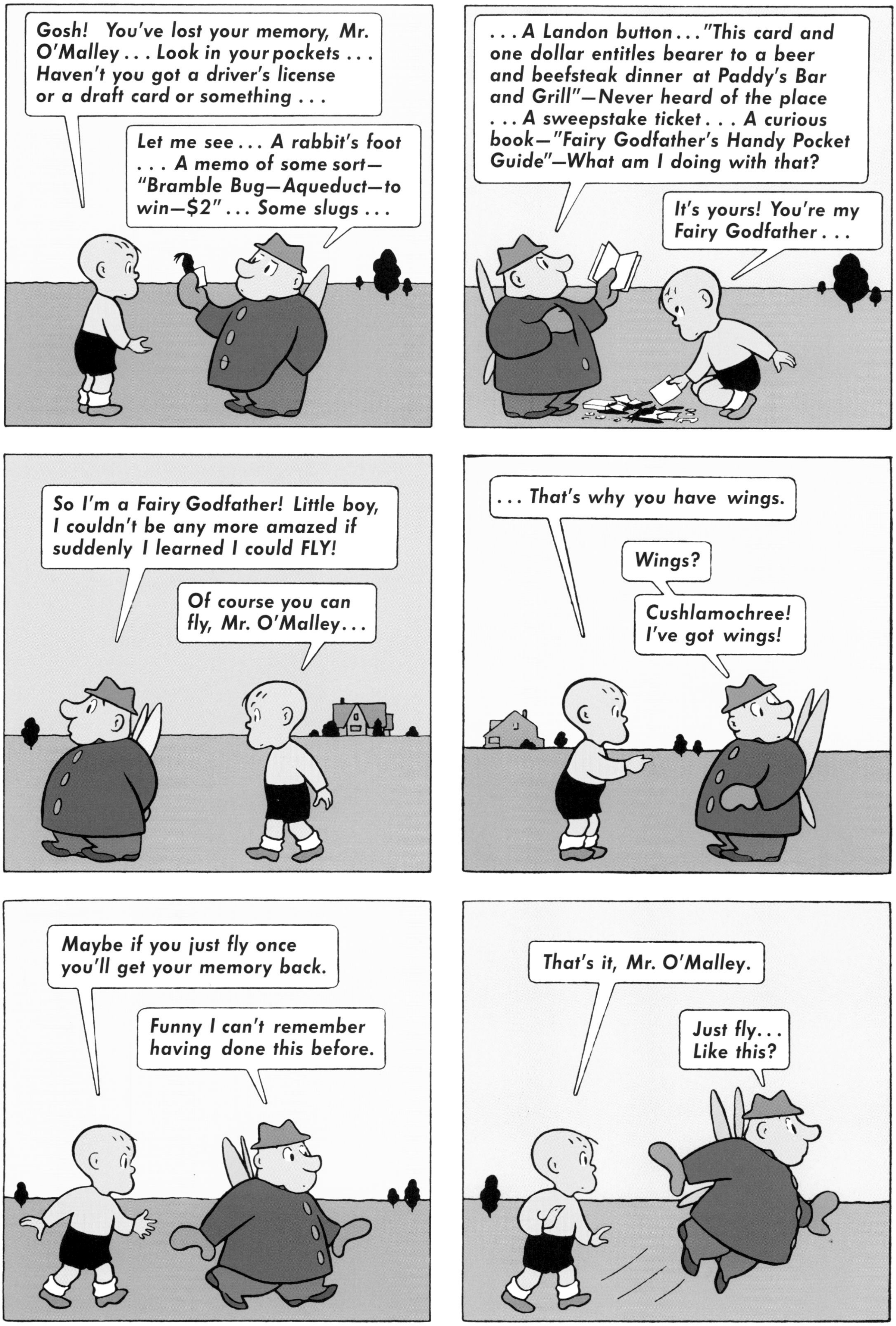
Gosh! You've lost your memory, Mr. O'Malley . . . Look in your pockets . . . Haven't you got a driver's license or a draft card or something . . .
Let me see . . . A rabbit's foot . . . A memo of some sort— "Bramble Bug—Aqueduct—to win—$2" . . . Some slugs . . .
. . . A Landon button . . . "This card and one dollar entitles bearer to a beer and beefsteak dinner at Paddy's Bar and Grill"—Never heard of the place . . . A sweepstake ticket . . . A curious book—"Fairy Godfather's Handy Pocket Guide"—What am I doing with that?
It's yours! You're my Fairy Godfather . . .
So I'm a Fairy Godfather! Little boy, I couldn't be any more amazed if suddenly I learned I could FLY!
Of course you can fly, Mr. O'Malley . . .
. . . That's why you have wings.
Wings?
Cushlamochree! I've got wings!
Maybe if you just fly once you'll get your memory back.
Funny I can't remember having done this before.
That's it, Mr. O'Malley.
Just fly . . . Like this?

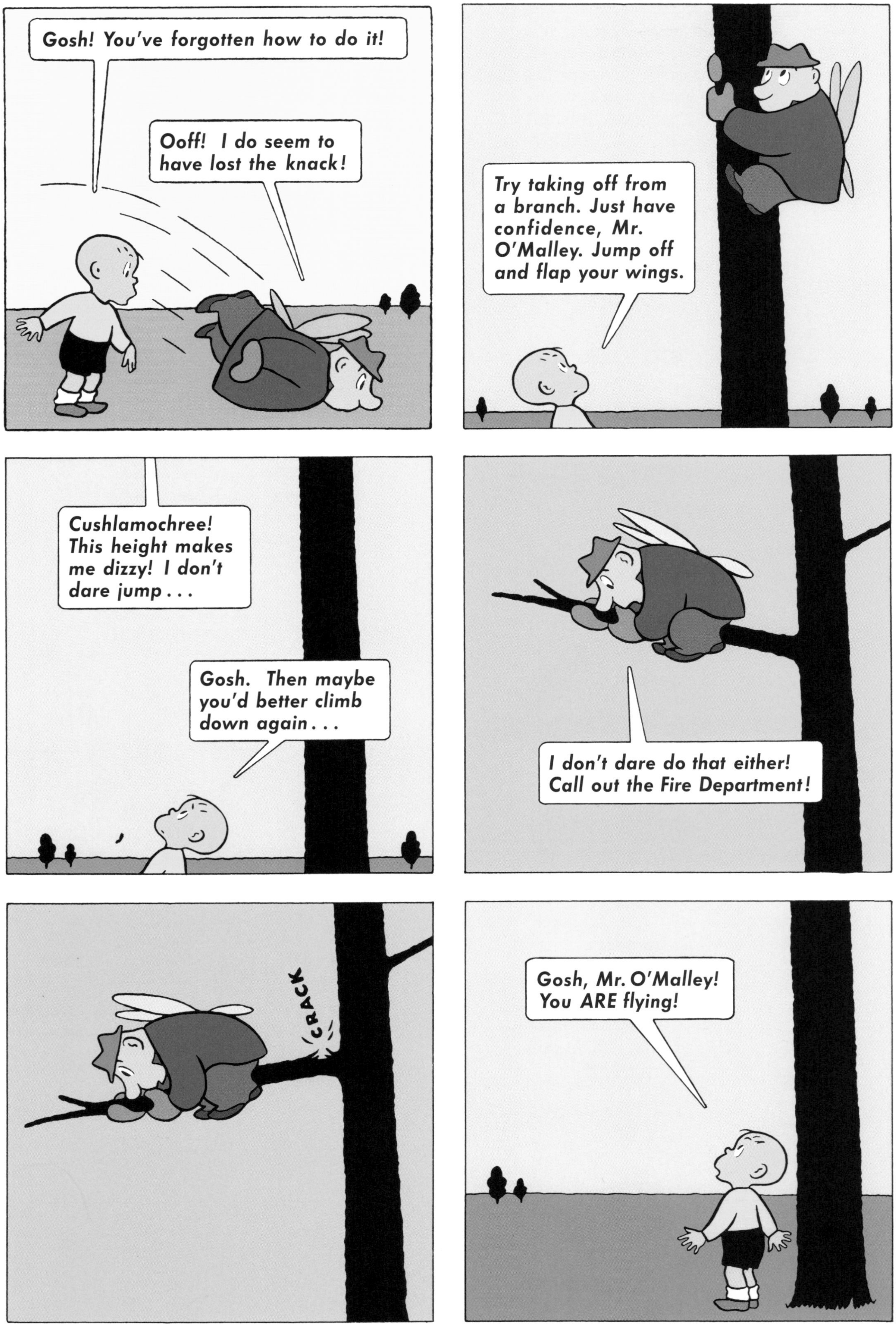
Gosh! You've forgotten how to do it!
Ooff! I do seem to have lost the knack!
Try taking off from a branch. Just have confidence, Mr. O'Malley. Jump off and flap your wings.
Cushlamochree! This height makes me dizzy! I don't dare jump...
Gosh. Then maybe you'd better climb down again...
I don't dare do that either! Call out the Fire Department!
CRACK
Gosh, Mr. O'Malley! You ARE flying!

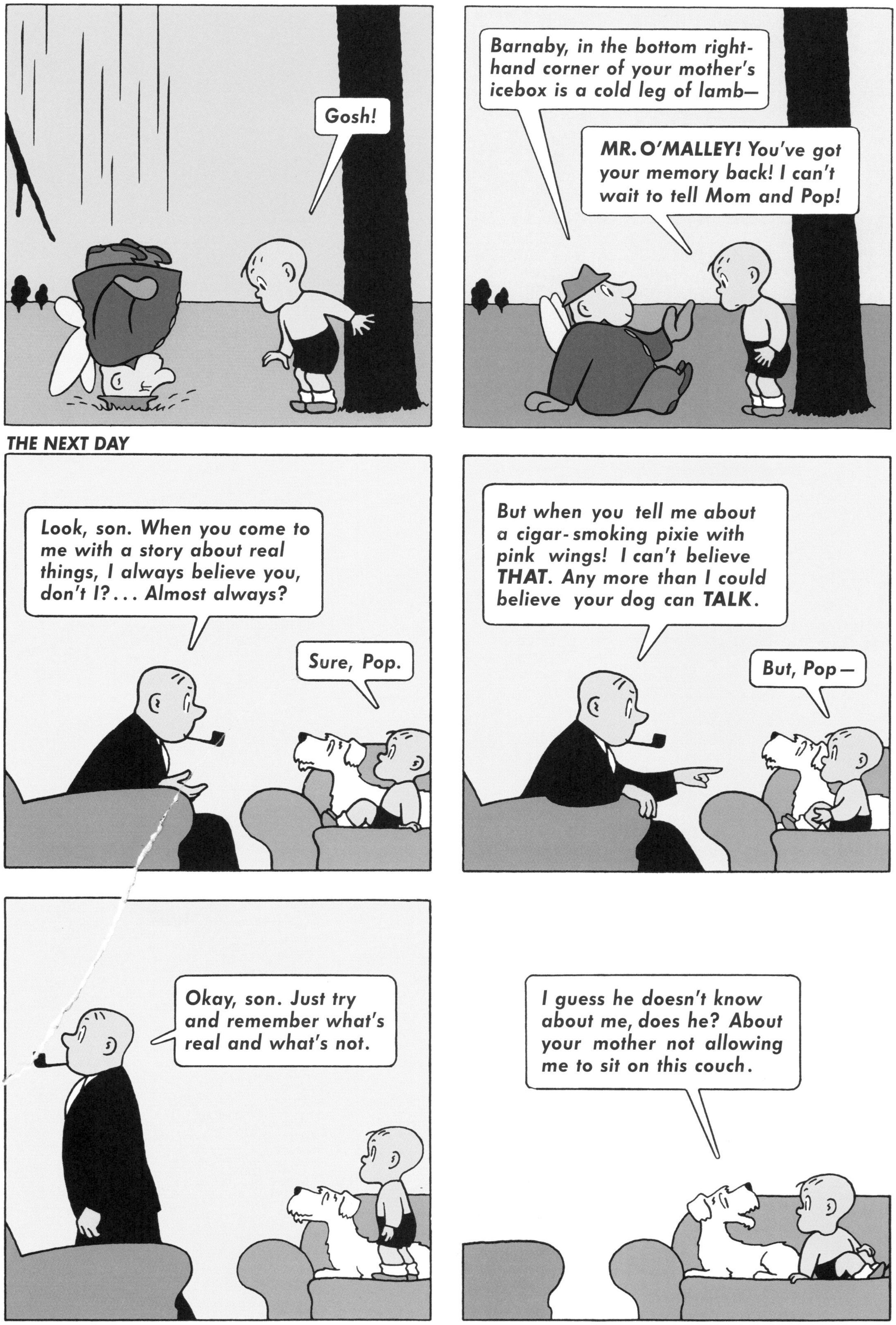
Gosh!
Barnaby, in the bottom right-hand corner of your mother's icebox is a cold leg of lamb—
MR. O'MALLEY! You've got your memory back! I can't wait to tell Mom and Pop!
THE NEXT DAY
Look, son. When you come to me with a story about real things, I always believe you, don't I?... Almost always?
Sure, Pop.
But when you tell me about a cigar-smoking pixie with pink wings! I can't believe THAT. Any more than I could believe your dog can TALK.
But, Pop—
Okay, son. Just try and remember what's real and what's not.
I guess he doesn't know about me, does he? About your mother not allowing me to sit on this couch.

There are many ways to travel through Lewis Trondheim's

A MAZE-ING

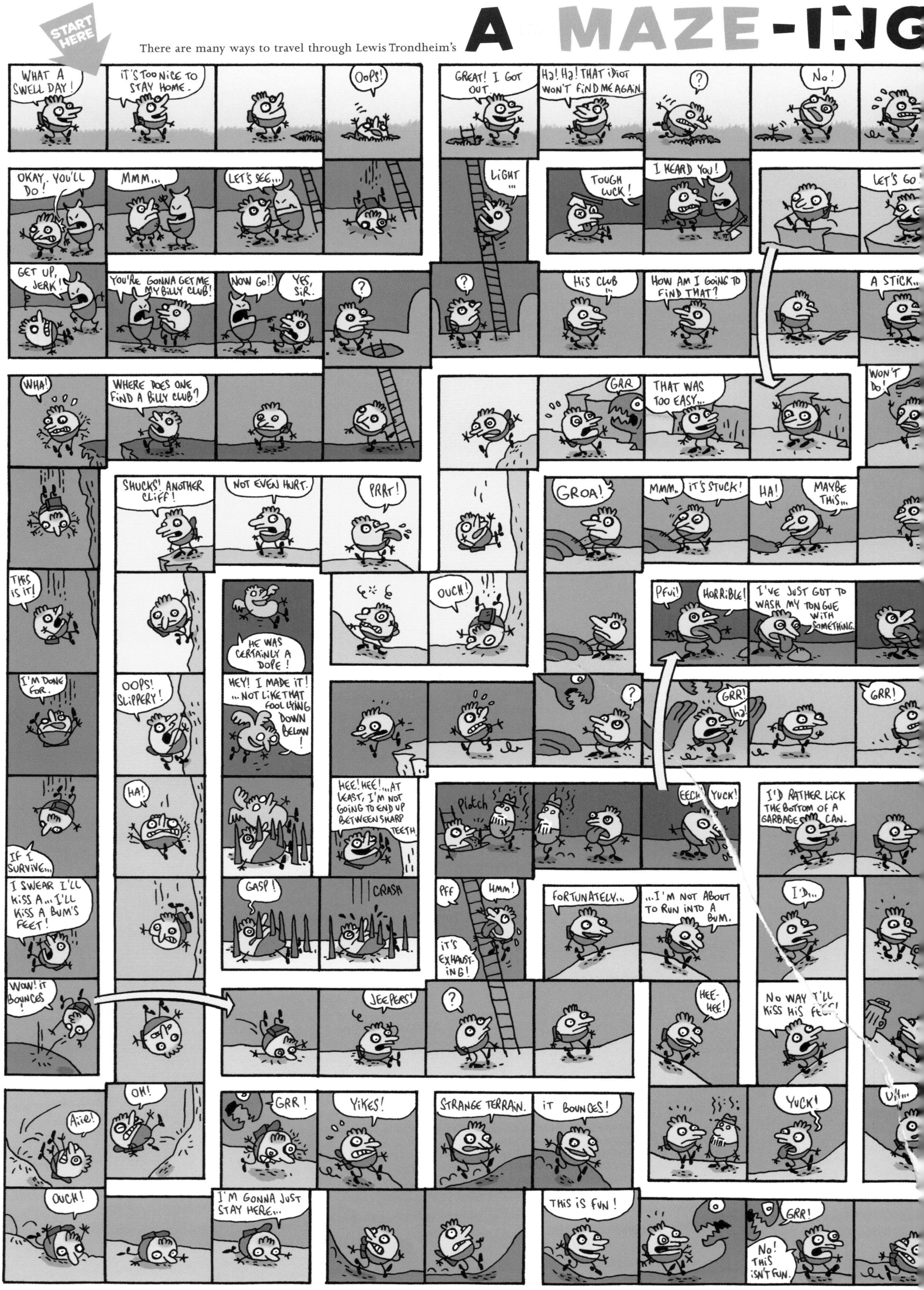
START HERE
WHAT A SWELL DAY!
IT'S TOO NICE TO STAY HOME.
OOPS!
GREAT! I GOT OUT.
HA! HA! THAT IDIOT WON'T FIND ME AGAIN.
?
NO!
OKAY. YOU'LL DO!
MMM...
LET'S SEE...
LIGHT ...
TOUGH LUCK!
I HEARD YOU!
LET'S GO
GET UP, JERK!
YOU'RE GONNA GET ME MY BILLY CLUB!
NOW GO!!
YES, SIR.
?
?
HIS CLUB ...
HOW AM I GOING TO FIND THAT?
A STICK...
WHA!
WHERE DOES ONE FIND A BILLY CLUB?
GAR
THAT WAS TOO EASY...
WON'T DO!
SHUCKS! ANOTHER CLIFF!
NOT EVEN HURT.
PRRT!
GROA!
MMM..
IT'S STUCK!
HA!
MAYBE THIS...
THIS IS IT!
HE WAS CERTAINLY A DOPE!
OUCH!
PFUI!
HORRIBLE!
I'VE JUST GOT TO WASH MY TONGUE WITH SOMETHING.
I'M DONE FOR.
OOPS! SLIPPERY!
HEY! I MADE IT! ...NOT LIKE THAT FOOL LYING DOWN BELOW!
?
GRR!
HA!
GRR!
IF I SURVIVE...
HA!
HEE! HEE! ...AT LEAST, I'M NOT GOING TO END UP BETWEEN SHARP TEETH
PLOTCH
EECH
YUCK!
I'D RATHER LICK THE BOTTOM OF A GARBAGE CAN.
I SWEAR I'LL KISS A... I'LL KISS A BUM'S FEET!
GASP!
CRASH
PFF
HMM!
IT'S EXHAUSTING!
FORTUNATELY...
...I'M NOT ABOUT TO RUN INTO A BUM.
I'D...
WOW! IT BOUNCES!
JEEPERS!
?
HEE-HEE!
NO WAY I'LL KISS HIS
AIIE!
OH!
GRR!
YIKES!
STRANGE TERRAIN.
IT BOUNCES!
YUCK!
UH...
OUCH!
I'M GONNA JUST STAY HERE...
THIS IS FUN!
GRR!
NO! THIS ISN'T FUN.

ADVENTURE

but there's only one way to reach the end and not be in the monster's clutches forever.

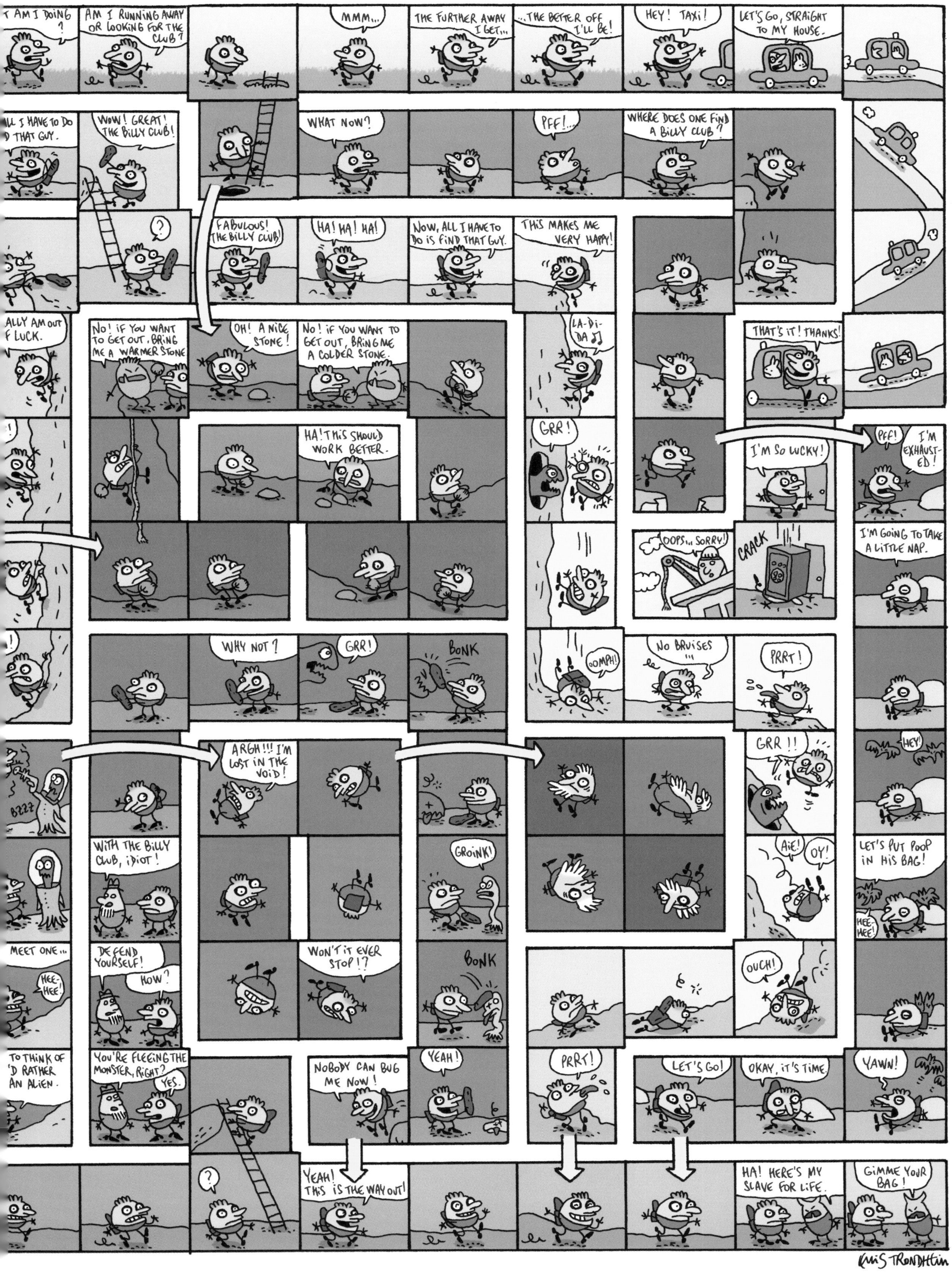

AM I RUNNING AWAY OR LOOKING FOR THE CLUB?
MMM...
THE FURTHER AWAY I GET...
...THE BETTER OFF I'LL BE!
HEY! TAXI!
LET'S GO, STRAIGHT TO MY HOUSE.
WOW! GREAT! THE BILLY CLUB!
WHAT NOW?
PFF!...
WHERE DOES ONE FIND A BILLY CLUB?
?
FABULOUS! THE BILLY CLUB!
HA! HA! HA!
NOW, ALL I HAVE TO DO IS FIND THAT GUY.
THIS MAKES ME VERY HAPPY!
NO! IF YOU WANT TO GET OUT, BRING ME A WARMER STONE
OH! A NICE STONE!
NO! IF YOU WANT TO GET OUT, BRING ME A COLDER STONE.
LA-DI-DA ♫
THAT'S IT! THANKS!
HA! THIS SHOULD WORK BETTER.
GRR!
I'M SO LUCKY!
PFF!
I'M EXHAUSTED!
OOPS... SORRY!
CRACK
I'M GOING TO TAKE A LITTLE NAP.
WHY NOT?
GRR!
BONK
OOMPH!
NO BRUISES !!!
PRRT!
ARGH!!! I'M LOST IN THE VOID!
GRR!!
HEY!
WITH THE BILLY CLUB, IDIOT!
GROINK!
AIE!
OY!
LET'S PUT POOP IN HIS BAG!
HEE-HEE!
HEE-HEE!
DEFEND YOURSELF!
HOW?
WON'T IT EVER STOP!?
BONK
OUCH!
YOU'RE FLEEING THE MONSTER, RIGHT?
YES.
NOBODY CAN BUG ME NOW!
YEAH!
PRRT!
LET'S GO!
OKAY, IT'S TIME.
YAWN!
?
YEAH! THIS IS THE WAY OUT!
HA! HERE'S MY SLAVE FOR LIFE.
GIMME YOUR BAG!
KRIS TRONDHEIM

marc rosenthal

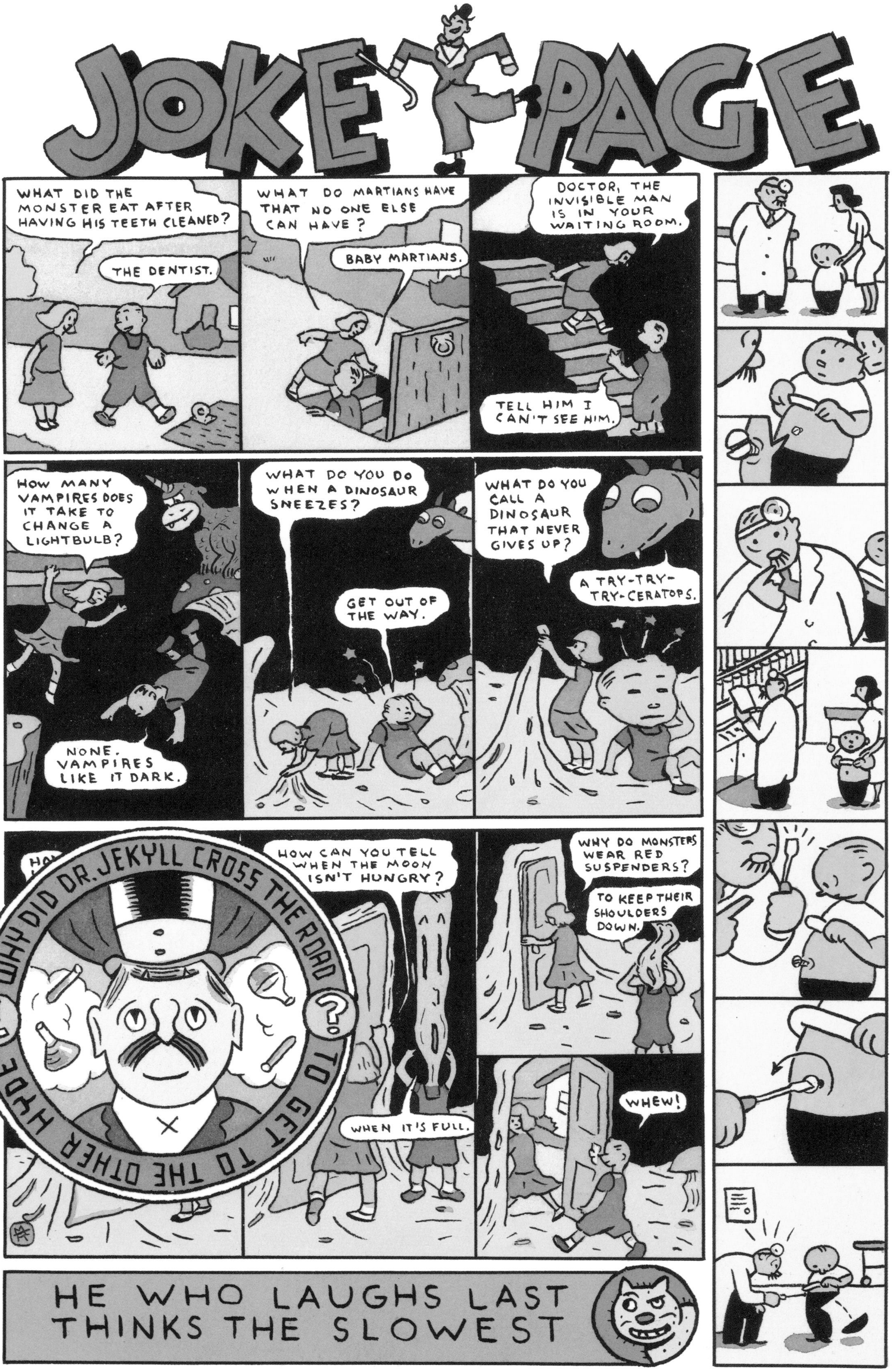
JOKE PAGE
WHAT DID THE MONSTER EAT AFTER HAVING HIS TEETH CLEANED?
THE DENTIST.
WHAT DO MARTIANS HAVE THAT NO ONE ELSE CAN HAVE?
BABY MARTIANS.
DOCTOR, THE INVISIBLE MAN IS IN YOUR WAITING ROOM.
TELL HIM I CAN'T SEE HIM.
HOW MANY VAMPIRES DOES IT TAKE TO CHANGE A LIGHTBULB?
NONE. VAMPIRES LIKE IT DARK.
WHAT DO YOU DO WHEN A DINOSAUR SNEEZES?
GET OUT OF THE WAY.
WHAT DO YOU CALL A DINOSAUR THAT NEVER GIVES UP?
A TRY-TRY-TRY-CERATOPS.
WHY DID DR. JEKYLL CROSS THE ROAD
TO GET TO THE OTHER HYDE
HOW CAN YOU TELL WHEN THE MOON ISN'T HUNGRY?
WHEN IT'S FULL.
WHY DO MONSTERS WEAR RED SUSPENDERS?
TO KEEP THEIR SHOULDERS DOWN.
WHEW!
HE WHO LAUGHS LAST THINKS THE SLOWEST

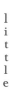

THE DAY I DISAPPEARED

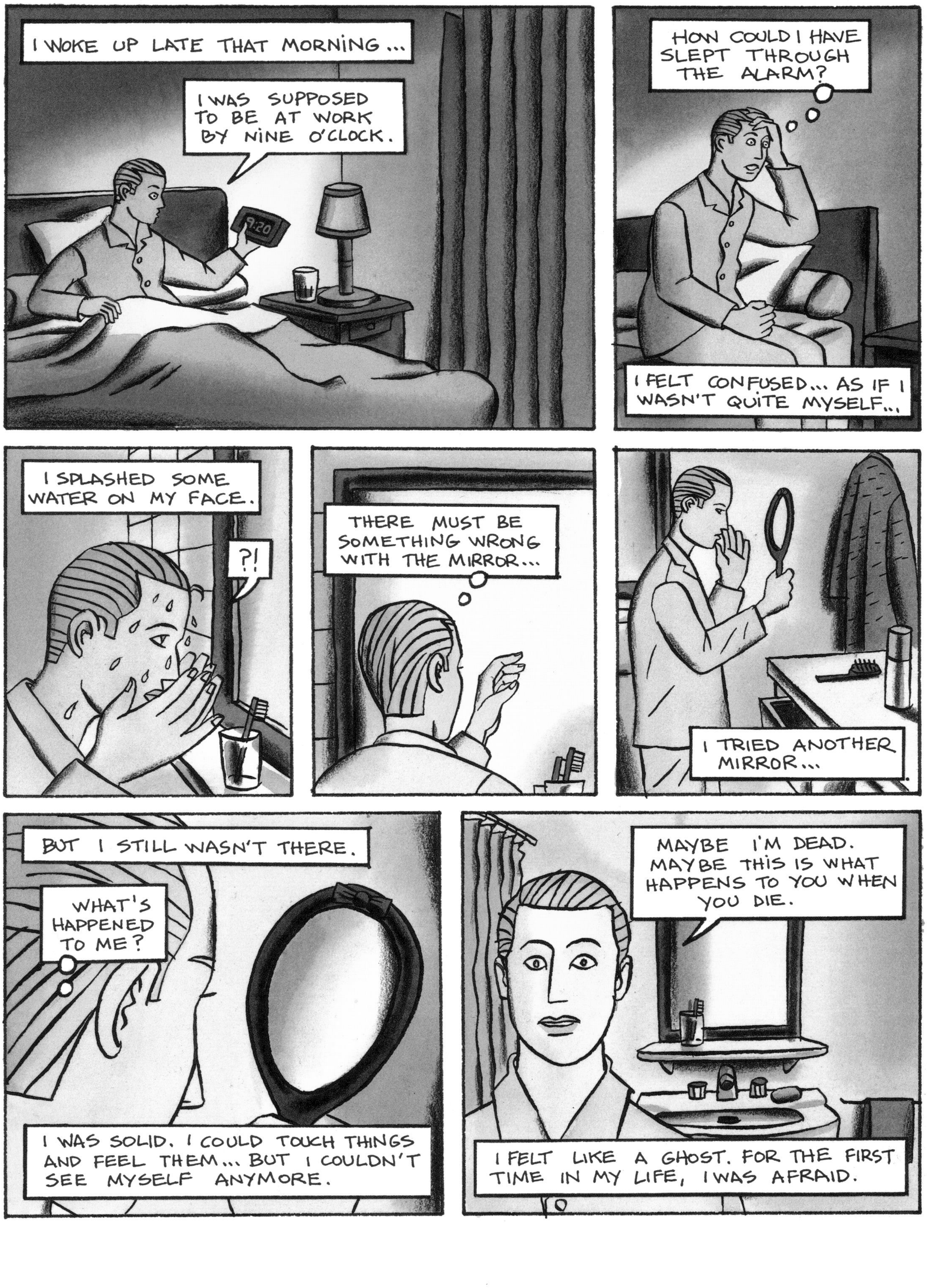
I WOKE UP LATE THAT MORNING...
I WAS SUPPOSED TO BE AT WORK BY NINE O'CLOCK.
9:20
HOW COULD I HAVE SLEPT THROUGH THE ALARM?
I FELT CONFUSED... AS IF I WASN'T QUITE MYSELF...
I SPLASHED SOME WATER ON MY FACE.
?!
THERE MUST BE SOMETHING WRONG WITH THE MIRROR...
I TRIED ANOTHER MIRROR...
BUT I STILL WASN'T THERE.
WHAT'S HAPPENED TO ME?
I WAS SOLID. I COULD TOUCH THINGS AND FEEL THEM... BUT I COULDN'T SEE MYSELF ANYMORE.
MAYBE I'M DEAD. MAYBE THIS IS WHAT HAPPENS TO YOU WHEN YOU DIE.
I FELT LIKE A GHOST. FOR THE FIRST TIME IN MY LIFE, I WAS AFRAID.

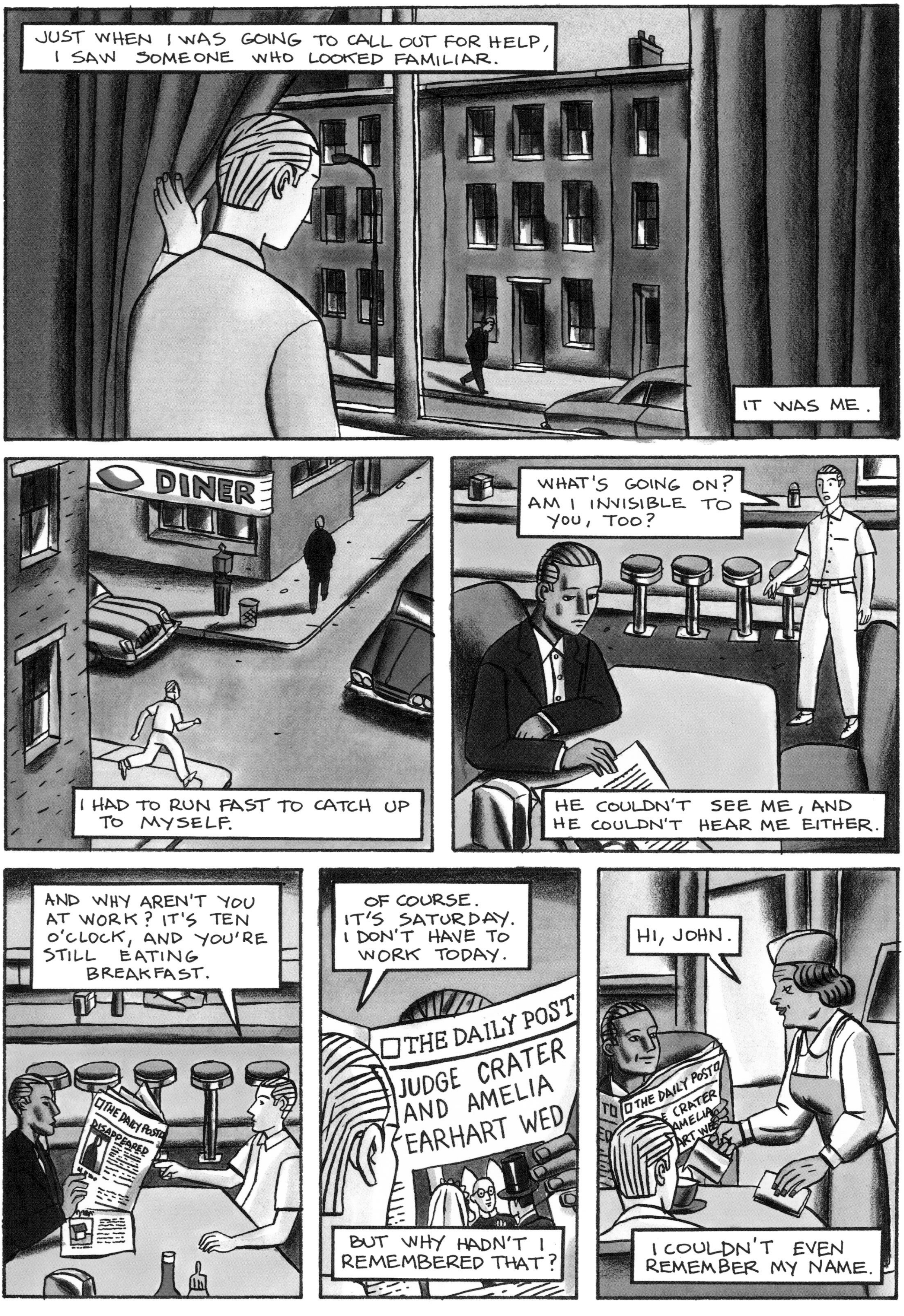
JUST WHEN I WAS GOING TO CALL OUT FOR HELP, I SAW SOMEONE WHO LOOKED FAMILIAR.
IT WAS ME.
DINER
I HAD TO RUN FAST TO CATCH UP TO MYSELF.
WHAT'S GOING ON? AM I INVISIBLE TO YOU, TOO?
HE COULDN'T SEE ME, AND HE COULDN'T HEAR ME EITHER.
AND WHY AREN'T YOU AT WORK? IT'S TEN O'CLOCK, AND YOU'RE STILL EATING BREAKFAST.
THE DAILY POST
DISAPPEARED
OF COURSE. IT'S SATURDAY. I DON'T HAVE TO WORK TODAY.
THE DAILY POST
JUDGE CRATER AND AMELIA EARHART WED
BUT WHY HADN'T I REMEMBERED THAT?
HI, JOHN.
THE DAILY POST
I COULDN'T EVEN REMEMBER MY NAME.

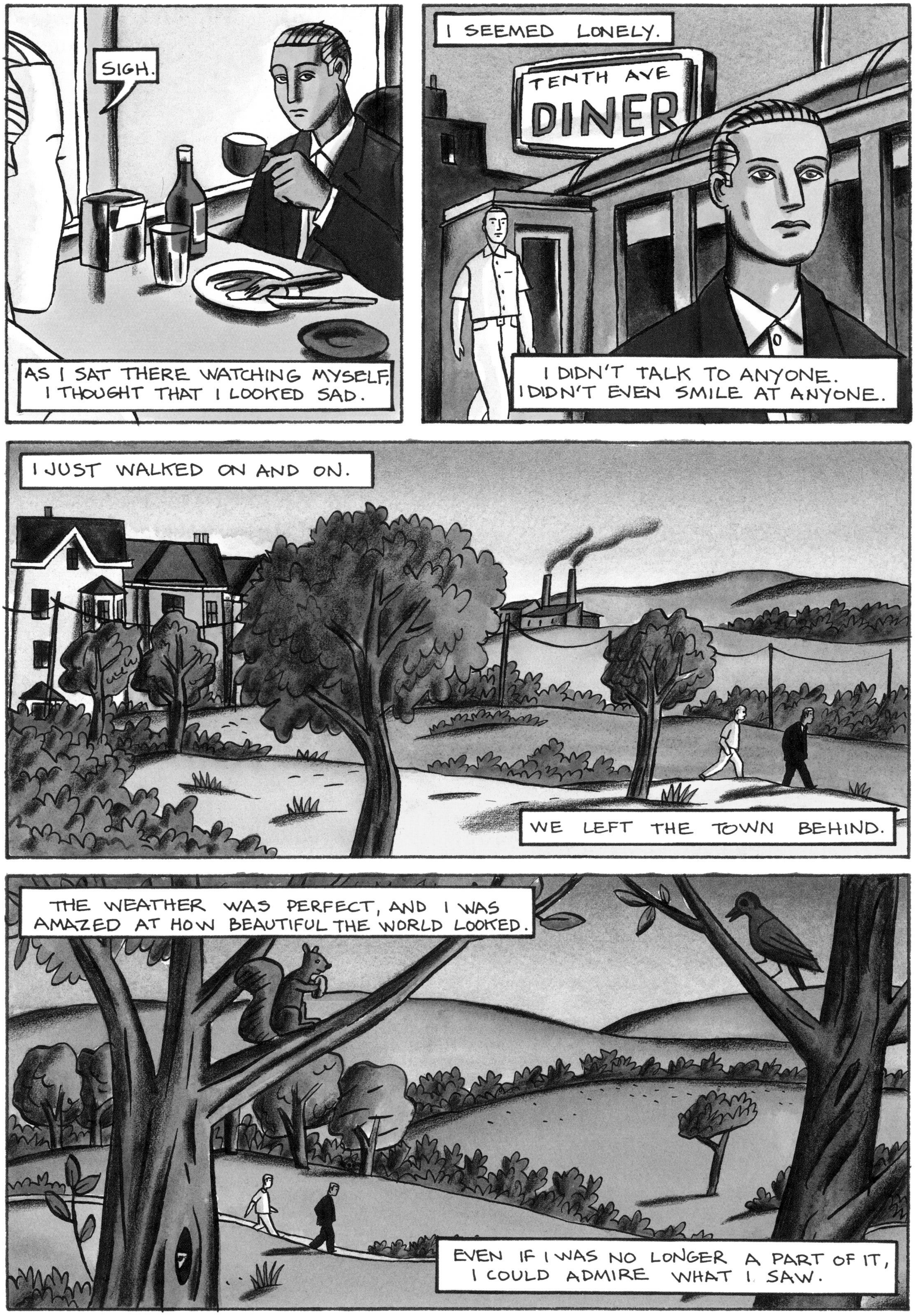
SIGH.
AS I SAT THERE WATCHING MYSELF, I THOUGHT THAT I LOOKED SAD.
I SEEMED LONELY.
TENTH AVE
DINER
I DIDN'T TALK TO ANYONE. I DIDN'T EVEN SMILE AT ANYONE.
I JUST WALKED ON AND ON.
WE LEFT THE TOWN BEHIND.
THE WEATHER WAS PERFECT, AND I WAS AMAZED AT HOW BEAUTIFUL THE WORLD LOOKED.
EVEN IF I WAS NO LONGER A PART OF IT, I COULD ADMIRE WHAT I SAW.

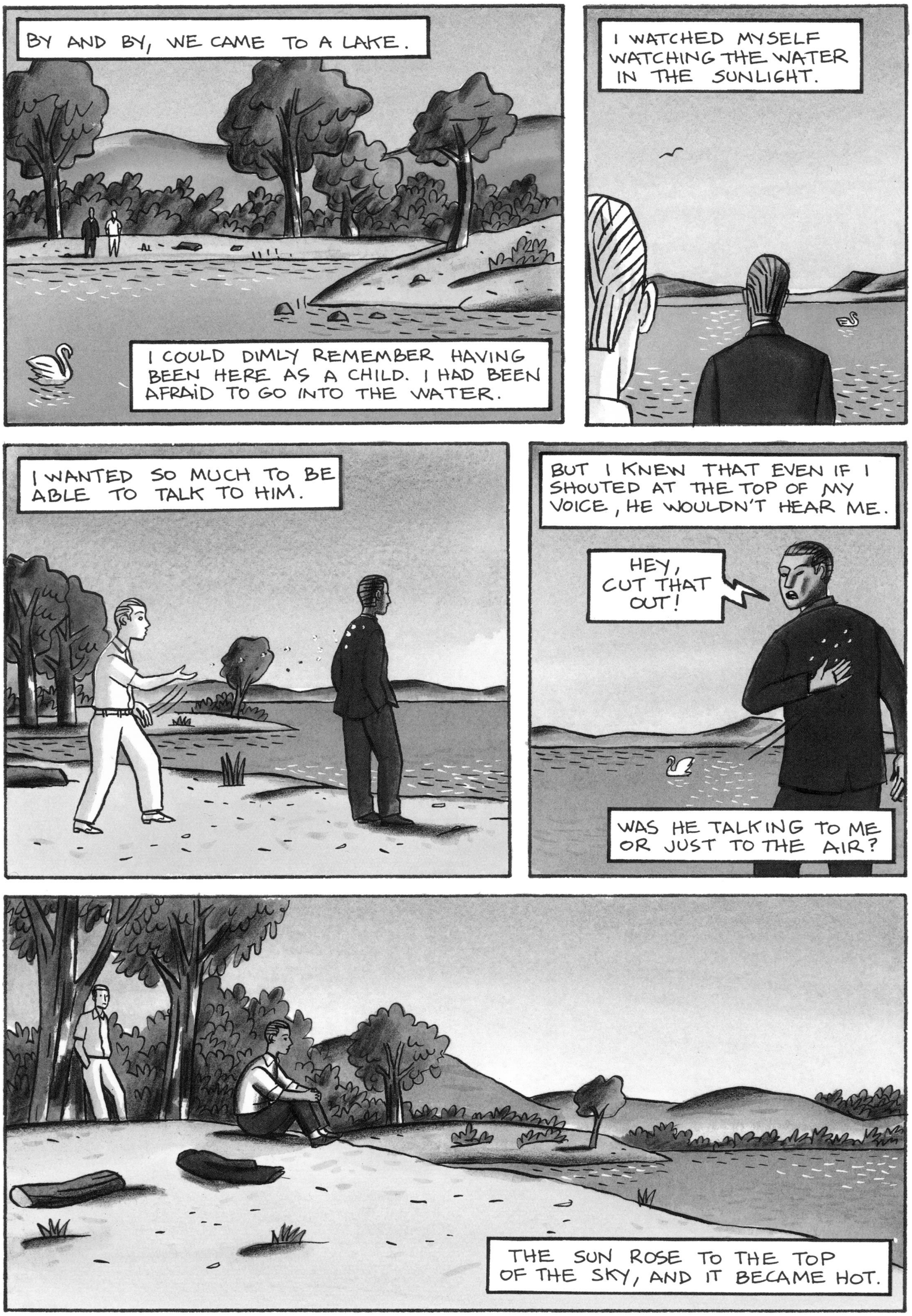
BY AND BY, WE CAME TO A LAKE.
I COULD DIMLY REMEMBER HAVING BEEN HERE AS A CHILD. I HAD BEEN AFRAID TO GO INTO THE WATER.
I WATCHED MYSELF WATCHING THE WATER IN THE SUNLIGHT.
I WANTED SO MUCH TO BE ABLE TO TALK TO HIM.
BUT I KNEW THAT EVEN IF I SHOUTED AT THE TOP OF MY VOICE, HE WOULDN'T HEAR ME.
HEY, CUT THAT OUT!
WAS HE TALKING TO ME OR JUST TO THE AIR?
THE SUN ROSE TO THE TOP OF THE SKY, AND IT BECAME HOT.

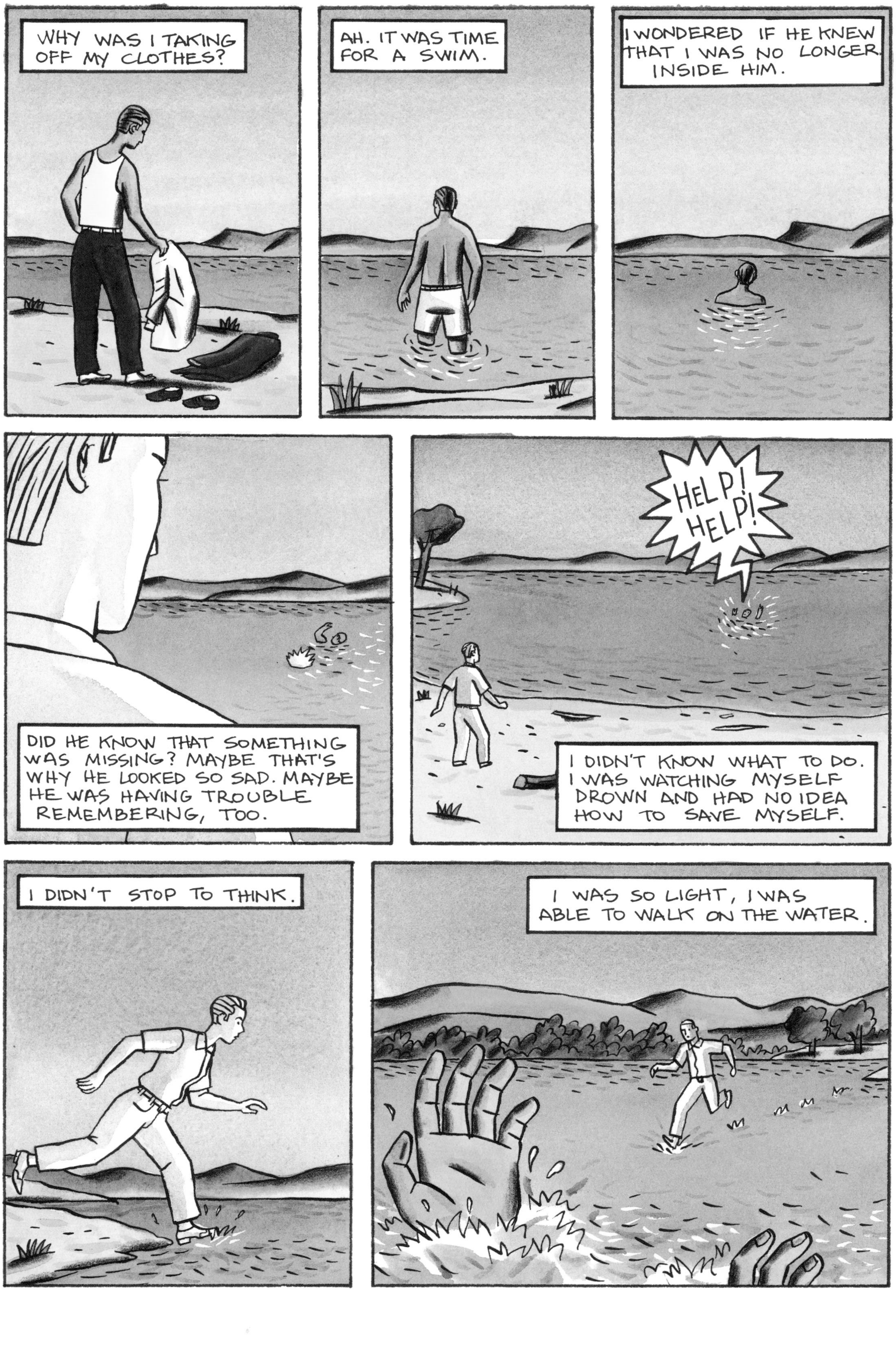
WHY WAS I TAKING OFF MY CLOTHES?
AH. IT WAS TIME FOR A SWIM.
I WONDERED IF HE KNEW THAT I WAS NO LONGER INSIDE HIM.
DID HE KNOW THAT SOMETHING WAS MISSING? MAYBE THAT'S WHY HE LOOKED SO SAD. MAYBE HE WAS HAVING TROUBLE REMEMBERING, TOO.
HELP! HELP!
I DIDN'T KNOW WHAT TO DO. I WAS WATCHING MYSELF DROWN AND HAD NO IDEA HOW TO SAVE MYSELF.
I DIDN'T STOP TO THINK.
I WAS SO LIGHT, I WAS ABLE TO WALK ON THE WATER.

I HAD TO DO SOMETHING.

IT WAS HORRIBLE TO SEE MYSELF SO AFRAID.

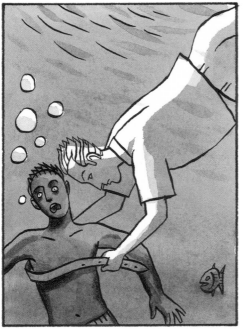

I WAS EXHAUSTED. I COLLAPSED ON THE GROUND AND FELL INTO A DEEP SLEEP.

WHEN I WOKE UP, I WAS ALONE.

I COULDN'T REMEMBER WHAT HAD HAPPENED.

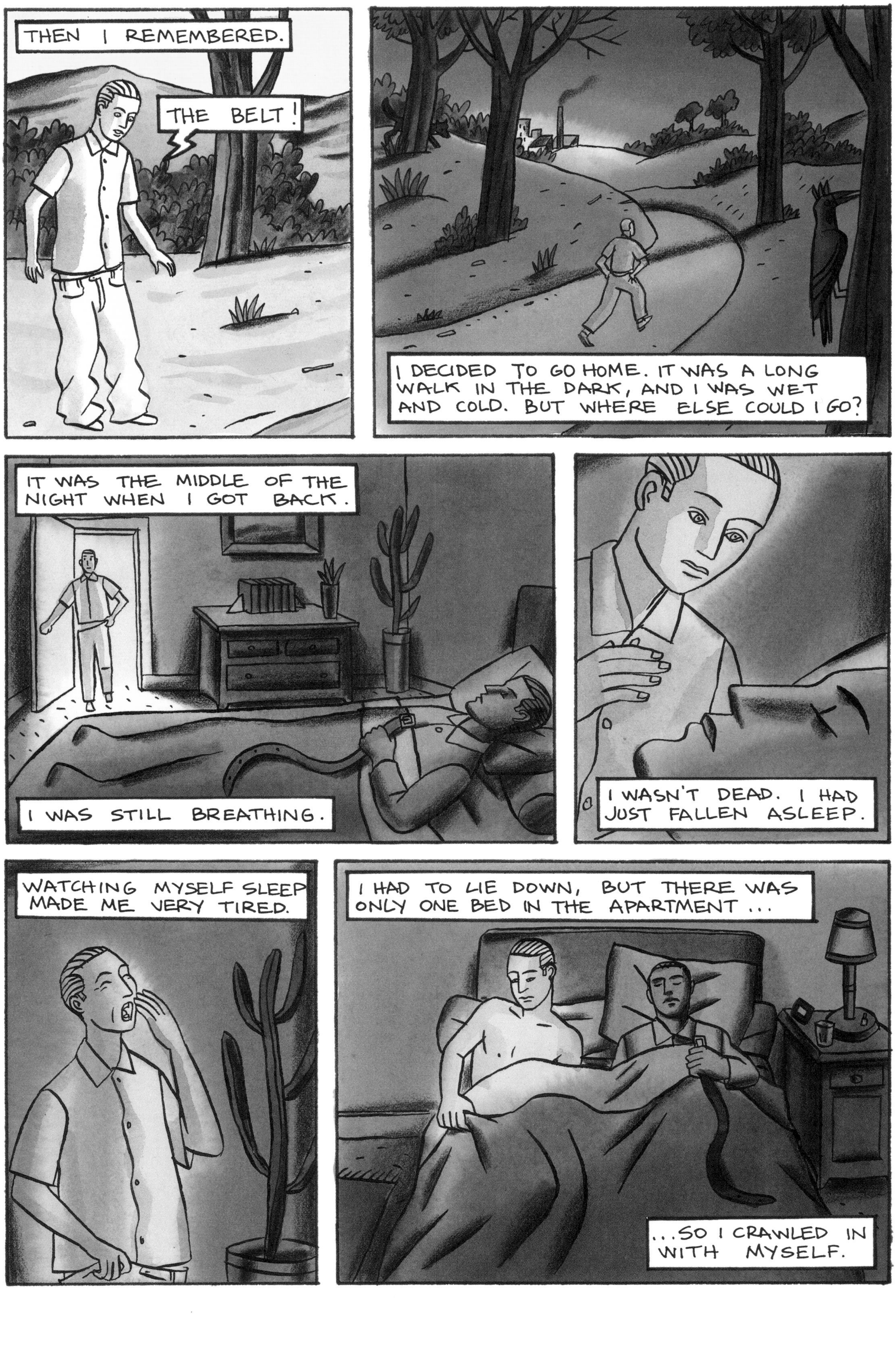
THEN I REMEMBERED.
THE BELT!
I DECIDED TO GO HOME. IT WAS A LONG WALK IN THE DARK, AND I WAS WET AND COLD. BUT WHERE ELSE COULD I GO?
IT WAS THE MIDDLE OF THE NIGHT WHEN I GOT BACK.
I WAS STILL BREATHING.
I WASN'T DEAD. I HAD JUST FALLEN ASLEEP.
WATCHING MYSELF SLEEP MADE ME VERY TIRED.
I HAD TO LIE DOWN, BUT THERE WAS ONLY ONE BED IN THE APARTMENT ...
...SO I CRAWLED IN WITH MYSELF.

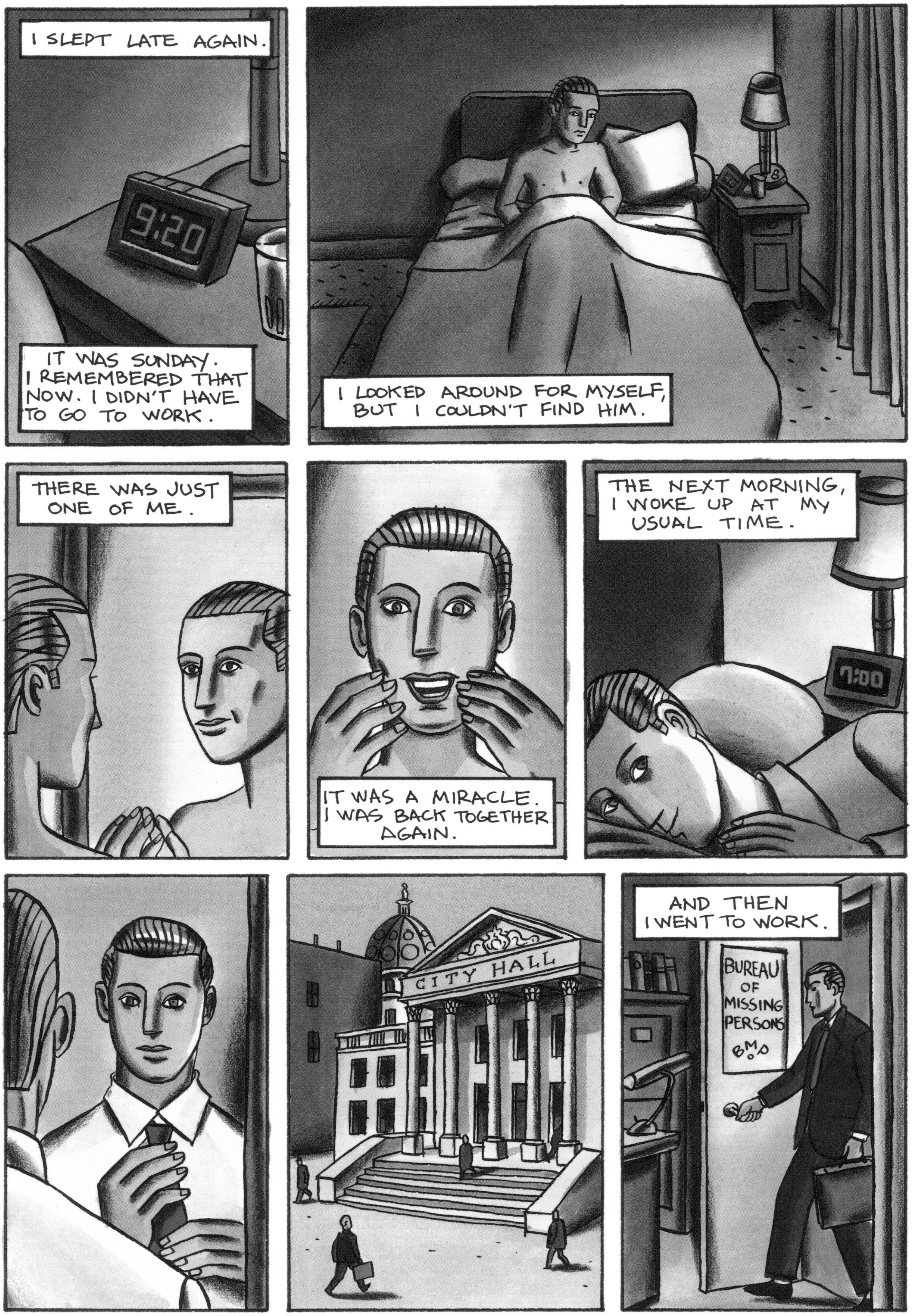
I SLEPT LATE AGAIN.
9:20
IT WAS SUNDAY. I REMEMBERED THAT NOW. I DIDN'T HAVE TO GO TO WORK.
I LOOKED AROUND FOR MYSELF, BUT I COULDN'T FIND HIM.
THERE WAS JUST ONE OF ME.
IT WAS A MIRACLE. I WAS BACK TOGETHER AGAIN.
THE NEXT MORNING, I WOKE UP AT MY USUAL TIME.
7:00
CITY HALL
AND THEN I WENT TO WORK.
BUREAU OF MISSING PERSONS

STRANGE PICTURE

One of our strange artists, François Roca, has made a picture even stranger than the others in this book. We found at least 22 odd things in this odd city. How many can YOU find?

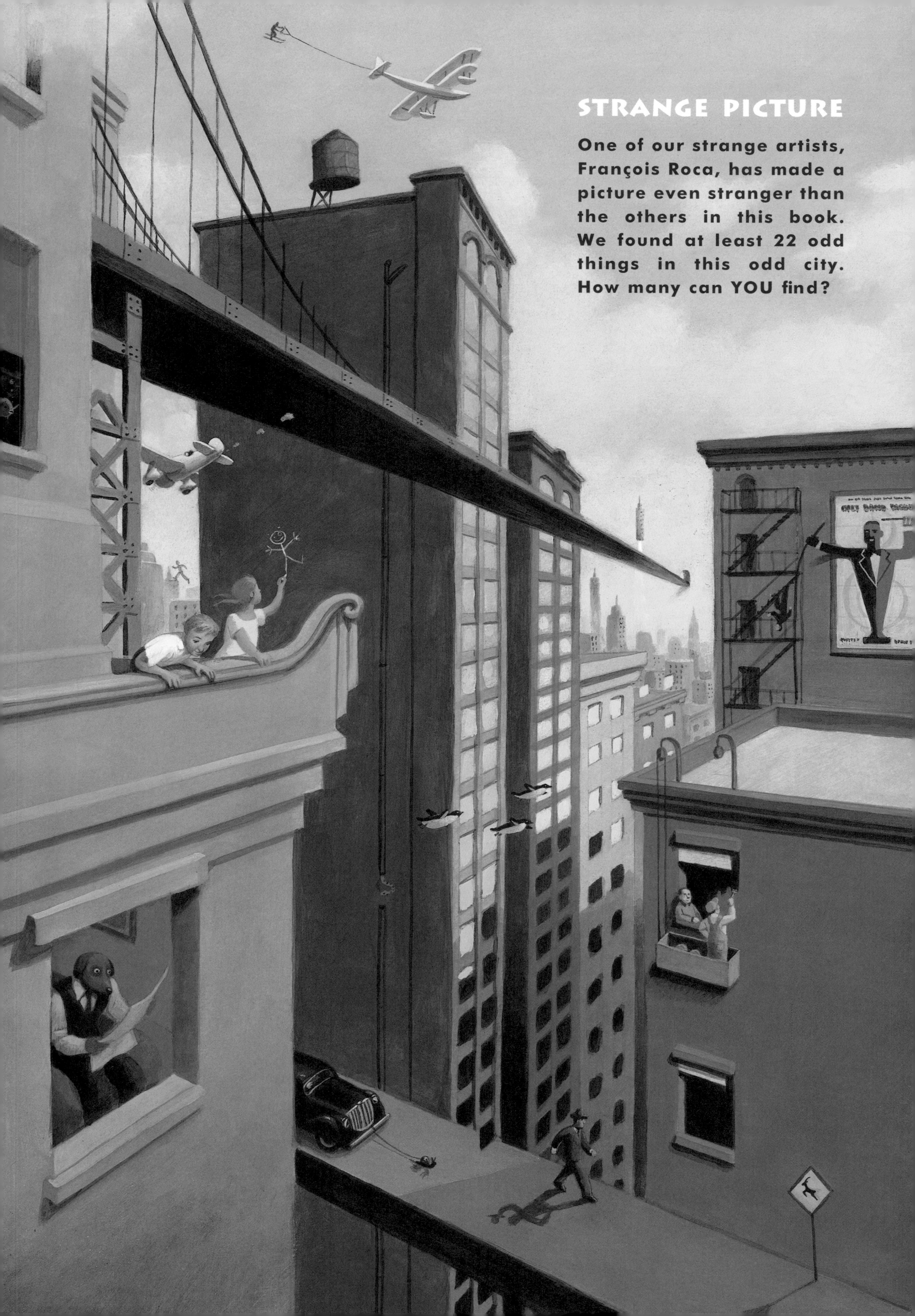

CONTRIBUTOR NOTES

CHARLES BURNS, who drew the front cover, was born in Washington, D.C., and now lives in Philadelphia with his wife, Susan, their two daughters, and a black cat named Iggy (also known as Ignatz). He is the creator of the ongoing comic book *Black Hole*, and an illustrator for magazines such as *Time* and *Rolling Stone*. A four-volume collection of his comics work is being published by Fantagraphics.

FRANÇOISE MOULY, born and raised in Paris, France, studied architecture at the Beaux Arts before coming to the United States at the age of 19. Beginning in 1980, she was the publisher, co-founder, and co-editor, with her husband, Art Spiegelman, of *RAW Magazine*, a comics anthology for adults. Françoise has been the art editor of *The New Yorker* since 1993. She recently edited and designed *Covering The New Yorker*, published by Abbeville Press. ART SPIEGELMAN, who wrote and drew *The Several Selves of Selby Sheldrake*, is the Pulitzer Prize–winning author of *MAUS: A Survivor's Tale*, an account of his parents' experiences in the Holocaust, as well as a children's book, *Open Me…I'm a Dog!* He is a staff writer and artist for *The New Yorker*. Born in Sweden, Art lives in Manhattan with Françoise and their two children, Nadja, 14, and Dashiell, 9.

MARTIN HANDFORD is the author of the popular *Where's Waldo?* series of books. He was born in Hampstead, England, where he lives with his wife, Elizabeth, and his two children, ages 4 and 2. Just like the little boy in his game, Martin has a house full of things he's collected, and never throws anything away. He is now at work on another book for the *Where's Waldo?* series.

MAURICE SENDAK, who wrote and drew *Cereal Baby Keller*, lives in Connecticut with his German shepherd, Max. Maurice won the 1964 Caldecott Medal for *Where the Wild Things Are*, and is the only American to win the international Hans Christian Andersen Award. He has designed sets and costumes for opera productions based on his *Where the Wild Things Are* and *Higglety Pigglety Pop!*, among others.

RICHARD McGUIRE is author and illustrator of *What Goes Around Comes Around, Night Becomes Day, The Orange Book*, and *What's Wrong With This Book?* His illustrations have appeared in *The New York Times* and many other major publications. His award-winning animated logo designs are seen regularly on PBS. Check out his recent web design, www.willing-to-try.com. Richard lives in Manhattan.

BARBARA McCLINTOCK has had three of her previous books win *The New York Times* Best Illustrated Books award. *Runaway Shadow* was inspired by one of her favorite strange stories, "The Shadow" by Hans Christian Andersen. Barbara is quite attached to her shadow and tries to treat it right. She is also very attached to her son, Larson, her friend David Johnson, and Kato, her possessive cat.

IAN FALCONER is a painter and illustrator whose work has appeared on the covers of *The New Yorker*. He has designed sets and costumes for the New York City Ballet, the San Francisco Opera, and the Royal Opera House, Covent Garden, among others. He won a Caldecott Honor for *Olivia*, his first children's book, published last year. *Pretty Ugly* is his first comic-book story. Ian lives in Manhattan.

DAVID SEDARIS was born in Johnson City, New York, and now lives in Paris, France. He is the author of four books, including *Naked* and *Me Talk Pretty One Day*. He writes plays with his sister Amy, one of which, *One Woman Shoe*, won an Obie award. He's also a regular contributor to Public Radio International's *This American Life*. *Pretty Ugly* was inspired by his sister Amy, who makes the world's scariest faces.

CLAUDE PONTI lives in Paris with his wife, their daughter, Adèle, and a cat. He is the creator of over fifty very popular children's books in France, as well as two books for grown-ups. He grew up in the northeast of France, where one can still find hoards of wild houses in the woods. Sometimes, when he can understand their language, they ask him to tell their stories. This is the story of a house he once knew.

JULES FEIFFER lives in Manhattan with his wife, Jenny Allen, a writer and stand-up comic. He has three daughters and one granddaughter. He is the author of fourteen collections of cartoons, two novels, a cartoon novel, nine plays and screenplays, and has won the Pulitzer Prize for editorial cartooning. His books for children include *Bark, George; The Man in the Ceiling; I Lost My Bear;* and, most recently, *I'm Not Bobby*.

POSY SIMMONDS grew up in Berkshire, England, and lives in London with her husband, Richard. She is the author and illustrator of the recent graphic novel *Gemma Bovery* and of the children's books *Lulu and the Flying Babies* and *FRED*, whose film version was nominated for an Oscar. *Mr. Frost* was inspired by the memory of several chilly days last January, when the central heating wasn't working.

KIM DEITCH has four books of comics in print, and has done comics for *Nickelodeon Magazine*. As a kid, he won drawing contests on the *Felix the Cat* and *Bozo the Clown* TV shows. He lives in Manhattan with his wife, Pamela, and two black-and-white cats, a boy named Zippy and a girl named Otto. One night, Pamela wanted him to tell her a bedtime story, and since she loves cats, he made up *These Cats Today!*

CROCKETT JOHNSON (1906–1975) is the pen name of David Johnson Leisk, who drew the *Barnaby* comic strip in the newspaper *PM* starting in 1942. It was later syndicated in fifty-two American newspapers and collected into the books *Barnaby* and *Barnaby and Mr. O'Malley*. He is the creator of the classic series of children's books *Harold and the Purple Crayon*.

LEWIS TRONDHEIM lives in Montpellier, France, with his two children, his wife (who is also the colorist of his comics), and one pet, a blue monster named Jean-Christophe, who is seven-and-a-half feet tall with four legs, three arms, ten mouths, and only two teeth. Though Lewis has done many books for kids, he found this maze so demanding that it will be a long, long time before he attempts another one.

MARC ROSENTHAL has illustrated many books for children, including *The Absentminded Fellow* and *The Runaway Beard*. With the Smithsonian Institution and the National Geographic Society, he helped create a traveling exhibition on geography for children called Earth 2U, which is now crossing the United States. Marc currently lives in the Berkshires with his wife, Eileen, his son, Willem, and Wayne the Cat.

JACQUES de LOUSTAL is the award-winning illustrator of many European comic albums. He is currently working on a comic story adapted from J. L. Coatalem's writings, as well as illustrations for Georges Simenon's novels. He likes to collaborate with writers, and was especially taken with Paul Auster's *The Day I Disappeared*. Jacques lives in Paris with his wife, their two daughters, and their Siamese cat.

PAUL AUSTER has published novels, screenplays, essays, memoirs, and poetry—including *The New York Trilogy, Smoke, The Invention of Solitude*, and *Timbuktu*. He is editor of the recent *I Thought My Father Was God and Other True Tales from NPR's National Story Project*. *The Day I Disappeared* is his first original comic book story. He lives in Brooklyn with his wife, Siri Hustvedt, their daughter, Sophie, and their dog, Jack.

FRANÇOIS ROCA is the illustrator of many French children's books, including *The Yellow Train*, published in the United States by Creative Editions. He is currently working on a book that tells the story of a man born without legs or arms, as well as an adaptation of *King Kong* for children. *Strange Picture* was inspired by the architecture of New York City. François lives in Paris.

KAZ was born in Hoboken, New Jersey, and now lives in Manhattan. He is the creator of *Underworld*, a weekly comic strip for adults, collected into four books published by Fantagraphics. Kaz has recently written for *Nickelodeon's SpongeBob SquarePants* cartoon show. His half-baked *Strange Cartoon Lesson* endpapers were designed to teach youngsters how to draw cartoons while driving them nuts.

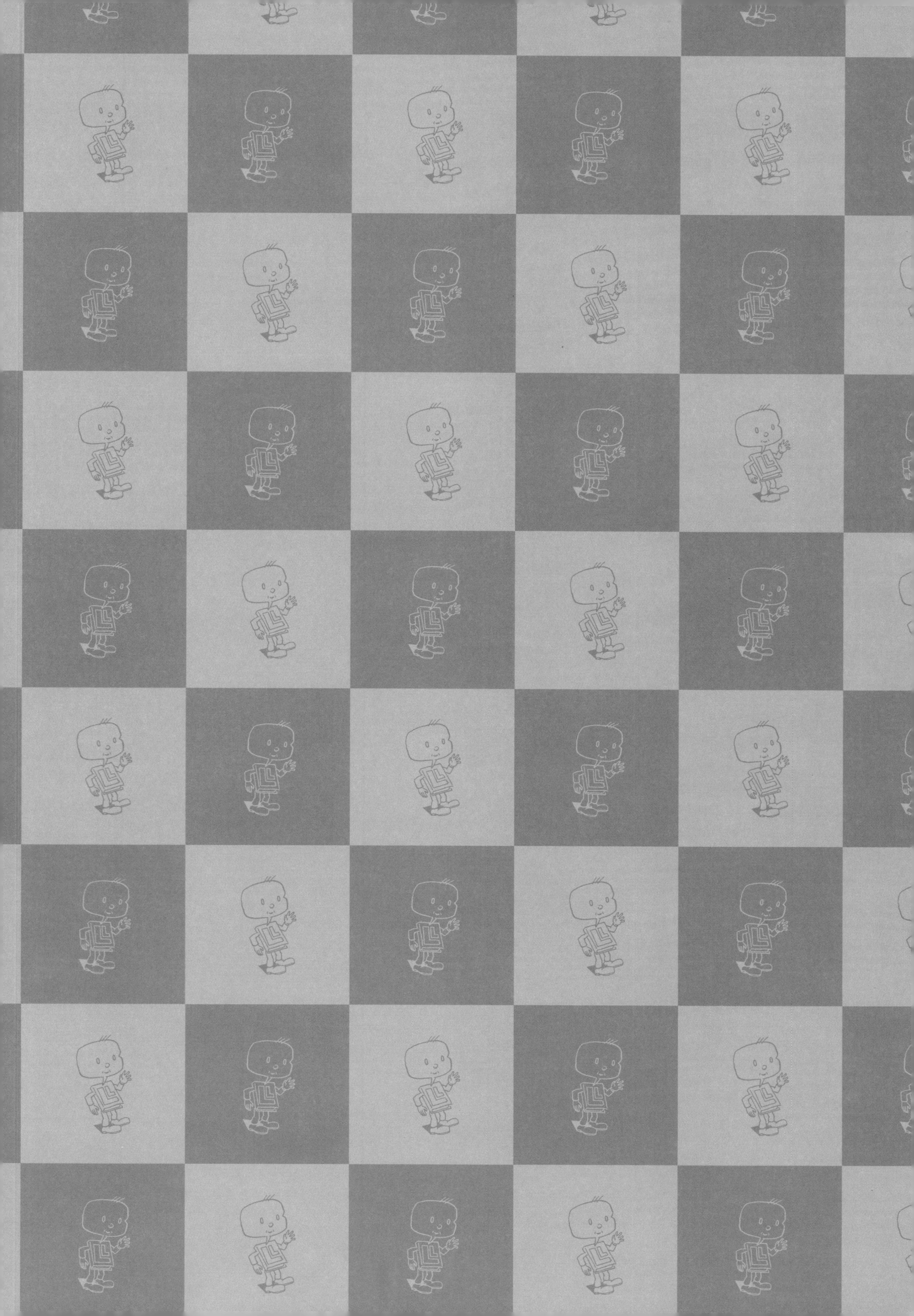

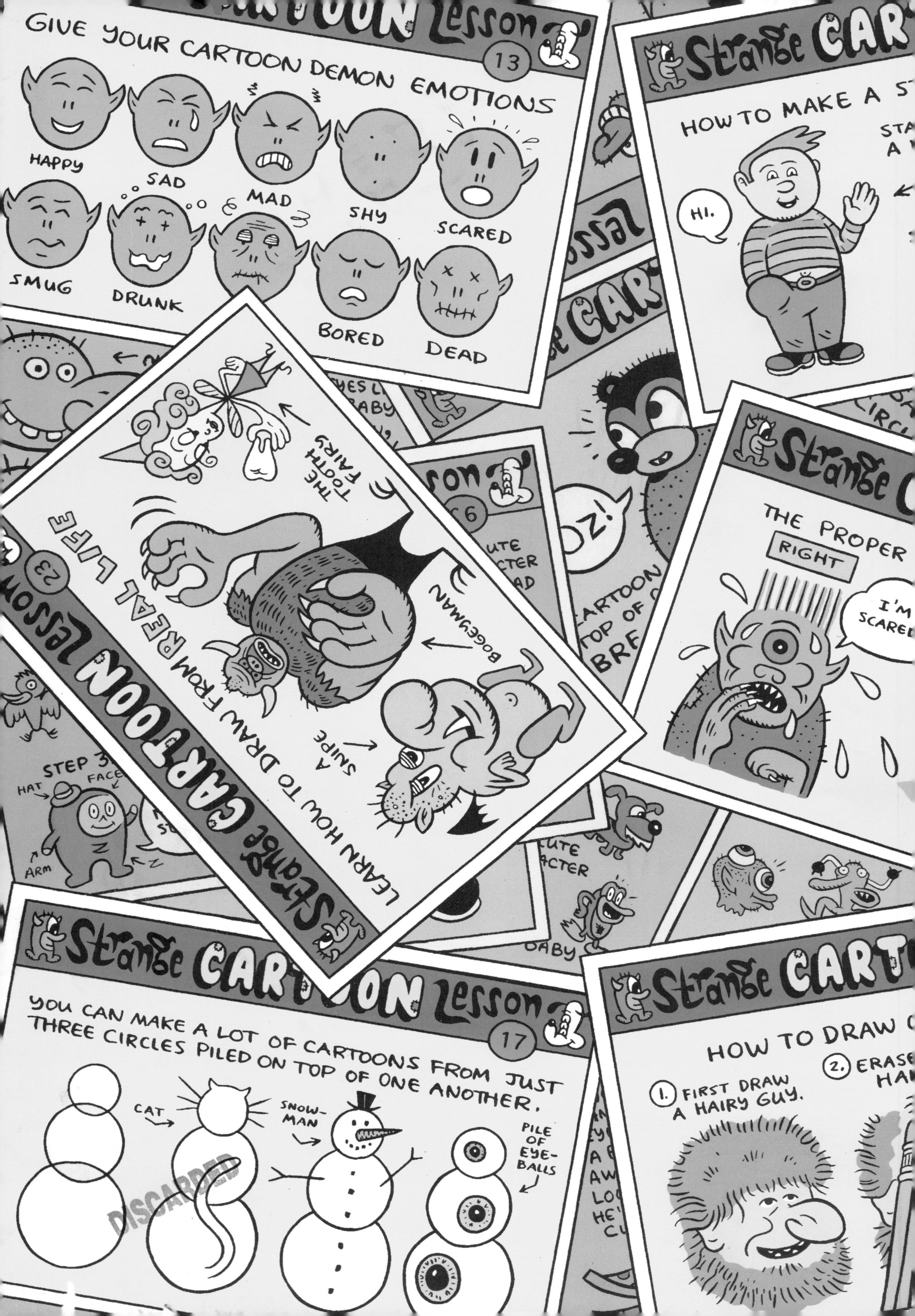
CARTOON Lesson
13
GIVE YOUR CARTOON DEMON EMOTIONS
HAPPY
SAD
MAD
SHY
SCARED
SMUG
DRUNK
BORED
DEAD
Strange CAR
HOW TO MAKE A ST
HI.
Strange CARTOON Lesson
23
LEARN HOW TO DRAW FROM REAL LIFE
THE TOOTH FAIRY
BOGEYMAN
A SNIPE
STEP 3
HAT
FACE
ARM
Strange C
THE PROPER
RIGHT
I'M SCARE
Strange CARTOON Lesson
17
YOU CAN MAKE A LOT OF CARTOONS FROM JUST THREE CIRCLES PILED ON TOP OF ONE ANOTHER.
CAT
SNOW-MAN
PILE OF EYE-BALLS
DISCARDED
Strange CART
HOW TO DRAW
1. FIRST DRAW A HAIRY GUY.
2. ERASE